WHITE NIGHT

A FAINT HEART [STORY]

FYODOR DOSTOEVSKY

Contents

First Night

It was a wonderful night, such a night as is only possible when we are young, dear reader. The sky was so starry, so bright that, looking at it, one could not help asking oneself whether ill-humoured and capricious people could live under such a sky. That is a youthful question too, dear reader, very youthful, but may the Lord put it more frequently into your heart!... Speaking of capricious and ill-humoured people, I cannot help recalling my moral condition all that day. From early morning I had been oppressed by a strange despondency. It suddenly seemed to me that I was lonely, that every one was forsaking me and going away from me. Of course, any one is entitled to ask who "every one" was. For though I had been living almost eight years in Petersburg I had hardly an acquaintance. But what did I want with acquaintances? I was acquainted with all Petersburg as it was; that was why I felt as though they were all deserting me when all Petersburg packed up and went to its summer villa. I felt afraid of being left alone, and for three whole days I wandered about the town in profound dejection, not knowing what to do with myself. Whether I walked in the Nevsky, went to the Gardens or sauntered on the embankment, there was not one face of those I had been accustomed to meet at the same time and place all the year. They, of course, do not know me, but I know them. I know them intimately, I have almost made a study of their faces, and am delighted when they are gay, and downcast when they are under a cloud. I have almost struck up a friendship with one old man whom I meet every blessed day, at the same hour in Fontanka. Such a grave, pensive countenance; he is always whispering to himself and brandishing his left arm, while in his right hand he holds a long gnarled stick with a gold knob. He even notices me and takes a warm interest in me. If I happen not to be at a certain time in the same spot in Fontanka, I am certain he feels disappointed. That is how it is that we almost bow to each other, especially when we are both in good humour. The other day, when we had not seen each other for two days and met on the third, we were actually touching our hats, but, realizing in time, dropped our hands and passed each other with a look of interest.

I know the houses too. As I walk along they seem to run forward in the streets to look out at me from every window, and almost to say: "Good-morning! How do you do? I am quite well, thank God, and I am to have a new storey in May," or, "How are you? I am being redecorated to-morrow;" or, "I was almost burnt down and had such a fright," and so on. I have my favourites among them, some are dear friends; one of them intends to be treated by the architect this summer. I shall go every day on purpose to see that the operation is not a failure. God forbid! But I shall never forget an incident with a very pretty little house of a light pink colour. It was such a charming little brick house, it looked so hospitably at me, and so proudly at its ungainly neighbours, that my heart rejoiced whenever I happened to pass it. Suddenly last week I walked along the street, and when I looked at my friend I heard a plaintive, "They are painting me yellow!" The villains! The barbarians! They had spared nothing, neither columns, nor cornices, and my poor little friend was as yellow as a canary. It almost made me bilious. And to this day I have not had the courage to visit my poor disfigured friend, painted the colour of the Celestial Empire.

So now you understand, reader, in what sense I am acquainted with all Petersburg.

I have mentioned already that I had felt worried for three whole days before I guessed the cause of my uneasiness. And I felt ill at ease in the street-this one had gone and that one had gone, and what had become of the other?-and at home I did not feel like myself either. For two evenings I was puzzling my brains to think what was amiss in my corner; why I felt so uncomfortable in it. And in perplexity I scanned my grimy green walls, my ceiling covered with a spider's web, the growth of which Matrona has so successfully encouraged. I looked over all my furniture, examined every chair, wondering whether the trouble lay there (for if one chair is not standing in the same position as it stood the day before, I am not myself). I looked at the window, but it was all in vain... I was not a bit the better for it! I even bethought me to send for Matrona, and was giving her some fatherly admonitions in regard to the spider's web and sluttishness in general; but she simply stared at me in amazement and went away without saying a word, so that the spider's web is comfortably hanging in its place to this day. I only at last this morning realized what was wrong. Aie! Why, they are giving me the slip and making off to their summer villas! Forgive the triviality of the expression, but I am in no mood for fine language... for everything that had been in Petersburg had gone or was going away for the holidays; for every respectable gentleman of dignified appearance who took a cab was at once transformed, in my eyes, into a respectable head of a household who after his daily duties were over, was making his way to the bosom of his family, to the summer villa; for all the passers-by had now quite a peculiar air which seemed to say to every one they met: "We are only here for the moment, gentlemen, and in another two hours we shall be going off to the summer villa." If a window opened after delicate fingers, white as snow, had tapped upon the pane, and the head of a pretty girl was thrust out, calling to a street-seller with pots of flowers-at once on the spot I fancied that those flowers were being bought not simply in order to enjoy the flowers and the spring in stuffy town lodgings, but because they would all be very soon moving into the country and could take the flowers with them. What is more, I made such progress in my new peculiar sort of investigation that I could distinguish correctly from the mere air of each in what summer villa he was living. The inhabitants of Kamenny and Aptekarsky Islands or of the Peterhof Road were marked by the studied elegance of their manner, their fashionable summer suits, and the fine carriages in which they drove to town. Visitors to Pargolovo and places further away impressed one at first sight by their reasonable and dignified air; the tripper to Krestovsky Island could be recognized by his look of irrepressible gaiety. If I chanced to meet a long procession of waggoners walking lazily with the reins in their hands beside waggons loaded with regular mountains of furniture, tables, chairs, ottomans and sofas and domestic utensils of all sorts, frequently with a decrepit cook sitting on the top of it all, guarding her master's property as though it were the apple of her eye; or if I saw boats heavily loaded with household goods crawling along the Neva or Fontanka to the Black River or the Islands-the waggons and the boats were multiplied tenfold, a hundredfold, in my eyes. I fancied that everything was astir and moving, everything was going in regular caravans to the summer villas. It seemed as though Petersburg threatened to become a wilderness, so that at last I felt ashamed, mortified and sad that I had nowhere to go for the holidays and no reason to go away. I was ready to go away with every waggon, to drive off with every gentleman of respectable appearance who took a cab; but no one-absolutely no one-invited me; it seemed they had forgotten me, as though really I were a stranger to them!

I took long walks, succeeding, as I usually did, in quite forgetting where I was, when I suddenly found myself at the city gates. Instantly I felt lighthearted, and I passed the barrier and walked between cultivated fields and meadows, unconscious of fatigue, and feeling only all over as though a burden were falling off my soul. All the passers-by gave me such friendly looks that they seemed almost greeting me, they all seemed so pleased at something. They were all smoking cigars, every one of them. And I felt pleased as I never had before. It was as though I had suddenly found myself in Italy-so strong was the effect of nature upon a half-sick townsman like me, almost stifling between city walls.

There is something inexpressibly touching in nature round Petersburg, when at the approach of spring she puts forth all her might, all the powers bestowed on her by Heaven, when she breaks into leaf, decks herself out and spangles herself with flowers.... Somehow I cannot help being reminded of a frail, consumptive girl, at whom one sometimes looks with compassion, sometimes with sympathetic love, whom sometimes one simply does not notice; though suddenly in one instant she becomes, as though by chance, inexplicably lovely and exquisite, and, impressed and intoxicated, one cannot help asking oneself what power made those sad, pensive eyes flash with such fire? What summoned the blood to those pale, wan cheeks? What bathed with passion those soft features? What set that bosom heaving? What so suddenly called strength, life and beauty into the poor girl's face, making it gleam with such a smile, kindle with such bright, sparkling laughter? You look round, you seek for some one, you conjecture.... But the moment passes, and next day you meet, maybe, the same pensive and preoccupied look as before, the same pale face, the same meek and timid movements, and even signs of remorse, traces of a mortal anguish and regret for the fleeting distraction.... And you grieve that the momentary beauty has faded so soon never to return, that it flashed upon you so treacherously, so vainly, grieve because you had not even time to love her.....

And yet my night was better than my day! This was how it happened.

I came back to the town very late, and it had struck ten as I was going towards my lodgings. My way lay along the canal embankment, where at that hour you never meet a soul. It is true that I live in a very remote part of the town. I walked along singing, for when I am happy I am always humming to myself like every happy man who has no friend or acquaintance with whom to share his joy. Suddenly I had a most unexpected adventure.

Leaning on the canal railing stood a woman with her elbows on the rail, she was apparently looking with great attention at the muddy water of the canal. She was wearing a very charming yellow hat and a jaunty little black mantle. "She's a girl, and I am sure she is dark," I thought. She did not seem to hear my footsteps, and did not even stir when I passed by with bated breath and loudly throbbing heart.

"Strange," I thought; "she must be deeply absorbed in something," and all at once I stopped as though petrified. I heard a muffled sob. Yes! I was not mistaken, the girl was crying, and a minute later I heard sob after sob. Good Heavens! My heart sank. And timid as I was with women, yet this was such a moment!... I turned, took a step towards her, and should certainly have pronounced the word "Madam!" if I had not known that that exclamation has been uttered a thousand times in every Russian society novel. It was only that reflection stopped me. But while I was seeking for a word, the girl came to herself, looked round, started, cast down her eyes and slipped by me along the embankment. I at once followed her; but she, divining this, left the embankment, crossed the road and walked along the pavement. I dared not cross the street after her. My heart was fluttering like a captured bird. All at once a chance came to my aid.

Along the same side of the pavement there suddenly came into sight, not far from the girl, a gentleman in evening dress, of dignified years, though by no means of dignified carriage; he was staggering and cautiously leaning against the wall. The girl flew straight as an arrow, with the timid haste one sees in all girls who do not want any one to volunteer to accompany them home at night, and no doubt the staggering gentleman would not have pursued her, if my good luck had not prompted him.

Suddenly, without a word to any one, the gentleman set off and flew full speed in pursuit of my unknown lady. She was racing like the wind, but the staggering gentleman was overtaking-overtook her. The girl uttered a shriek, and ... I bless my luck for the excellent knotted stick, which happened on that occasion to be in my right hand. In a flash I was on the other side of the street; in a flash the obtrusive gentleman had taken in the position, had grasped the irresistible argument, fallen back without a word, and only when we were very far away protested against my action in rather vigorous language. But his words hardly reached us.

"Give me your arm," I said to the girl. "And he won't dare to annoy us further."

She took my arm without a word, still trembling with excitement and terror. Oh, obtrusive gentleman! How I blessed you at that moment! I stole a glance at her, she was very charming and dark-I had guessed right.

On her black eyelashes there still glistened a tear-from her recent terror or her former grief-I don't know. But there was already a gleam of a smile on her lips. She too stole a glance at me, faintly blushed and looked down.

"There, you see; why did you drive me away? If I had been here, nothing would have happened...."

"But I did not know you; I thought that you too...."

"Why, do you know me now?"

"A little! Here, for instance, why are you trembling?"

"Oh, you are right at the first guess!" I answered, delighted that my girl had intelligence; that is never out of place in company with beauty. "Yes, from the first glance you have guessed the sort of man you have to do with. Precisely; I am shy with women, I am agitated, I don't deny it, as much so as you were a minute ago when that gentleman alarmed you. I am in some alarm now. It's like a dream, and I never guessed even in my sleep that I should ever talk with any woman."

"What? Really?..."

"Yes; if my arm trembles, it is because it has never been held by a pretty little hand like yours. I am a complete stranger to women; that is, I have never been used to them. You see, I am alone.... I don't even know how to talk to them. Here, I don't know now whether I have not said something silly to you! Tell me frankly; I assure you beforehand that I am not quick to take offence?..."

"No, nothing, nothing, quite the contrary. And if you insist on my speaking frankly, I will tell you that women like such timidity; and if you want to know more, I like it too, and I won't drive you away till I get home."

"You will make me," I said, breathless with delight, "lose my timidity, and then farewell to all my chances...."

"Chances! What chances–of what? That's not so nice."

"I beg your pardon, I am sorry, it was a slip of the tongue; but how can you expect one at such a moment to have no desire...."

"To be liked, eh?"

"Well, yes; but do, for goodness' sake, be kind. Think what I am! Here, I am twenty-six and I have never seen any one. How can I speak well, tactfully, and to the point? It will seem better to you when I have told you everything openly.... I don't know how to be silent when my heart is speaking. Well, never mind.... Believe me, not one woman, never, never! No acquaintance of any sort! And I do nothing but dream every day that at last I shall meet some one. Oh, if only you knew how often I have been in love in that way...."

"How? With whom?..."

"Why, with no one, with an ideal, with the one I dream of in my sleep. I make up regular romances in my dreams. Ah, you don't know me! It's true, of course, I have met two or three women, but what sort of women were they? They were all landladies, that.... But I shall make you laugh if I tell you that I have several times thought of speaking, just simply speaking, to some aristocratic lady in the street, when she is alone, I need hardly say; speaking to her, of course, timidly, respectfully, passionately; telling her that I am perishing in solitude, begging her not to send me away; saying that I have no chance of making the acquaintance of any woman; impressing upon her that it is a positive duty for a woman not to repulse so timid a prayer from such a luckless man as me. That, in fact, all I ask is, that she should say two or three sisterly words with sympathy, should not repulse me at first sight; should take me on trust and listen to what I say; should laugh at me if she likes, encourage me, say two words to me, only two words, even though we never meet again afterwards!... But you are laughing; however, that is why I am telling you...."

"Don't be vexed; I am only laughing at your being your own enemy, and if you had tried you would have succeeded, perhaps, even though it had been in the street; the simpler the better.... No kind-hearted woman, unless she were stupid or, still more, vexed about something at the moment, could bring herself to send you away without those two words which you ask for so timidly.... But what am I saying? Of course she would take you for a madman. I was judging by myself; I know a good deal about other people's lives."

"Oh, thank you," I cried; "you don't know what you have done for me now!"

"I am glad! I am glad! But tell me how did you find out that I was the sort of woman with whom... well, whom you think worthy... of attention and friendship... in fact, not a landlady as you say? What made you decide to come up to me?"

"What made me?... But you were alone; that gentleman was too insolent; it's night. You must admit that it was a duty...."

"No, no; I mean before, on the other side-you know you meant to come up to me."

"On the other side? Really I don't know how to answer; I am afraid to.... Do you know I have been happy to-day? I walked along singing; I went out into the country; I have never had such happy moments. You... perhaps it was my fancy.... Forgive me for referring to it; I fancied you were crying, and I... could not bear to hear it... it made my heart ache.... Oh, my goodness! Surely I might be troubled about you? Surely there was no harm in feeling brotherly compassion for you.... I beg your pardon, I said compassion.... Well, in short, surely you would not be offended at my involuntary impulse to go up to you?..."

"Stop, that's enough, don't talk of it," said the girl, looking down, and pressing my hand. "It's my fault for having spoken of it; but I am glad I was not mistaken in you.... But here I am home; I must go down this turning, it's two steps from here.... Good-bye, thank you!..."

"Surely ... surely you don't mean ... that we shall never see each other again?... Surely this is not to be the end?"

"You see," said the girl, laughing, "at first you only wanted two words, and now.... However, I won't say anything... perhaps we shall meet...."

"I shall come here to-morrow," I said. "Oh, forgive me, I am already making demands...."

"Yes, you are not very patient... you are almost insisting."

"Listen, listen!" I interrupted her. "Forgive me if I tell you something else.... I tell you what, I can't help coming here to-morrow, I am a dreamer; I have so little real life that I look upon such moments as this now, as so rare, that I cannot help going over such moments again in my dreams. I shall be dreaming of you all night, a whole week, a whole year. I shall certainly come here to-morrow, just here to this place, just at the same hour, and I shall be happy remembering to-day. This place is dear to me already. I have already two or three such places in Petersburg. I once shed tears over memories... like you.... Who knows, perhaps you were weeping ten minutes ago over some memory.... But, forgive me, I have forgotten myself again; perhaps you have once been particularly happy here...."

"Very good," said the girl, "perhaps I will come here to-morrow, too, at ten o'clock. I see that I can't forbid you.... The fact is, I have to be here; don't imagine that I am making an appointment with you; I tell you beforehand that I have to be here on my own account. But... well, I tell you straight out, I don't mind if you do come. To begin with, something unpleasant might happen as it did to-day, but never mind that.... In short, I should simply like to see you... to say two words to you. Only, mind, you must not think the worse of me now! Don't think I make appointments so lightly.... I shouldn't make it except that.... But let that be my secret! Only a compact beforehand...."

"A compact! Speak, tell me, tell me all beforehand; I agree to anything, I am ready for anything," I cried delighted. "I answer for myself, I will be obedient, respectful... you know me...."

"It's just because I do know you that I ask you to come to-morrow," said the girl, laughing. "I know you perfectly. But mind you will come on the condition, in the first place (only be good, do what I ask–you see, I speak frankly), you won't fall in love with me.... That's impossible, I assure you. I am ready for friendship; here's my hand.... But you mustn't fall in love with me, I beg you!"

"I swear," I cried, gripping her hand....

"Hush, don't swear, I know you are ready to flare up like gunpowder. Don't think ill of me for saying so. If only you knew.... I, too, have no one to whom I can say a word, whose advice I can ask. Of course, one does not look for an adviser in the street; but you are an exception. I know you as though we had been friends for twenty years.... You won't deceive me, will you?..."

"You will see... the only thing is, I don't know how I am going to survive the next twenty-four hours."

"Sleep soundly. Good-night, and remember that I have trusted you already. But you exclaimed so nicely just now, 'Surely one can't be held responsible for every feeling, even for brotherly sympathy!' Do you know, that was so nicely said, that the idea struck me at once, that I might confide in you?"

"For God's sake do; but about what? What is it?"

"Wait till to-morrow. Meanwhile, let that be a secret. So much the better for you; it will give it a faint flavour of romance. Perhaps I will tell you to-morrow, and perhaps not.... I will talk to you a little more beforehand; we will get to know each other better...."

"Oh yes, I will tell you all about myself to-morrow! But what has happened? It is as though a miracle had befallen me.... My God, where am I? Come, tell me aren't you glad that you were not angry and did not drive me away at the first moment, as any other woman would have done? In two minutes you have made me happy for ever. Yes, happy; who knows, perhaps, you have reconciled me with myself, solved my doubts!... Perhaps such moments come upon me.... But there I will tell you all about it to-morrow, you shall know everything, everything...."

"Very well, I consent; you shall begin...."

"Agreed."

"Good-bye till to-morrow!"

"Till to-morrow!"

And we parted. I walked about all night; I could not make up my mind to go home. I was so happy.... To-morrow!

Second Night

Well, so you have survived!" she said, pressing both my hands.

"I've been here for the last two hours; you don't know what a state I have been in all day."

"I know, I know. But to business. Do you know why I have come? Not to talk nonsense, as I did yesterday. I tell you what, we must behave more sensibly in future. I thought a great deal about it last night."

"In what way–in what must we be more sensible? I am ready for my part; but, really, nothing more sensible has happened to me in my life than this, now."

"Really? In the first place, I beg you not to squeeze my hands so; secondly, I must tell you that I spent a long time thinking about you and feeling doubtful to-day."

"And how did it end?"

"How did it end? The upshot of it is that we must begin all over again, because the conclusion I reached to-day was that I don't know you at all; that I behaved like a baby last night, like a little girl; and, of course, the fact of it is, that it's my soft heart that is to blame–that is, I sang my own praises, as one always does in the end when one analyses one's conduct. And therefore to correct my mistake, I've made up my mind to find out all about you minutely. But as I have no one from whom I can find out anything, you must tell me everything fully yourself. Well, what sort of man are you? Come, make haste–begin–tell me your whole history."

"My history!" I cried in alarm. "My history! But who has told you I have a history? I have no history...."

"Then how have you lived, if you have no history?" she interrupted, laughing.

"Absolutely without any history! I have lived, as they say, keeping myself to myself, that is, utterly alone—alone, entirely alone. Do you know what it means to be alone?"

"But how alone? Do you mean you never saw any one?"

"Oh no, I see people, of course; but still I am alone."

"Why, do you never talk to any one?"

"Strictly speaking, with no one."

"Who are you then? Explain yourself! Stay, I guess: most likely, like me you have a grandmother. She is blind and will never let me go anywhere, so that I have almost forgotten how to talk; and when I played some pranks two years ago, and she saw there was no holding me in, she called me up and pinned my dress to hers, and ever since we sit like that for days together; she knits a stocking, though she's blind, and I sit beside her, sew or read aloud to her–it's such a queer habit, here for two years I've been pinned to her...."

"Good Heavens! what misery! But no, I haven't a grandmother like that."

"Well, if you haven't why do you sit at home?..."

"Listen, do you want to know the sort of man I am?"

"Yes, yes!"

"In the strict sense of the word?"

"In the very strictest sense of the word."

"Very well, I am a type!

"Type, type! What sort of type?" cried the girl, laughing, as though she had not had a chance of laughing for a whole year. "Yes, it's very amusing talking to you. Look, here's a seat, let us sit down. No one is passing here, no one will hear us, and–begin your history. For it's no good your telling me, I know you have a history; only you are concealing it. To begin with, what is a type?"

"A type? A type is an original, it's an absurd person!" I said, infected by her childish laughter. "It's a character. Listen; do you know what is meant by a dreamer?"

"A dreamer! Indeed I should think I do know. I am a dreamer myself. Sometimes, as I sit by grandmother, all sorts of things come into my head. Why, when one begins dreaming one lets one's fancy run away with one–why, I marry a Chinese Prince!... Though sometimes it is a good thing to dream! But, goodness knows! Especially when one has something to think of apart from dreams," added the girl, this time rather seriously.

"Excellent! If you have been married to a Chinese Emperor, you will quite understand me. Come, listen.... But one minute, I don't know your name yet."

"At last! You have been in no hurry to think of it!"

"Oh, my goodness! It never entered my head, I felt quite happy as it was...."

"My name is Nastenka."

"Nastenka! And nothing else?"

"Nothing else! Why, is not that enough for you, you insatiable person?"

"Not enough? On the contrary, it's a great deal, a very great deal, Nastenka; you kind girl, if you are Nastenka for me from the first."

"Quite so! Well?"

"Well, listen, Nastenka, now for this absurd history."

I sat down beside her, assumed a pedantically serious attitude, and began as though reading from a manuscript:–

"There are, Nastenka, though you may not know it, strange nooks in Petersburg. It seems as though the same sun as shines for all Petersburg people does not peep into those spots, but some other different new one, bespoken expressly for those nooks, and it throws a different light on everything. In these corners, dear Nastenka, quite a different life is lived, quite unlike the life that is surging round us, but such as perhaps exists in some unknown realm, not among us in our serious, over-serious, time. Well, that life is a mixture of something purely fantastic, fervently ideal, with something (alas! Nastenka) dingily prosaic and ordinary, not to say incredibly vulgar."

"Foo! Good Heavens! What a preface! What do I hear?"

"Listen, Nastenka. (It seems to me I shall never be tired of calling you Nastenka.) Let me tell you that in these corners live strange people–dreamers. The dreamer–if you want an exact definition–is not a human being, but a creature of an intermediate sort. For the most part he settles in some inaccessible corner, as though hiding from the light of day; once he slips into his corner, he grows to it like a snail, or, anyway, he is in that respect very much like that remarkable creature, which is an animal and a house both at once, and is called a tortoise. Why do you suppose he is so fond of his four walls, which are invariably painted green, grimy, dismal and reeking unpardonably of tobacco smoke? Why is it that when this absurd gentleman is visited by one of his few acquaintances (and he ends by getting rid of all his friends), why does this absurd person meet him with such embarrassment, changing countenance and overcome with confusion, as though he had only just committed some crime within his four walls; as though he had been forging counterfeit notes, or as though he were writing verses to be sent to a journal with an anonymous letter, in which he states that the real poet is dead, and that his friend thinks it his sacred duty to publish his things? Why, tell me, Nastenka, why is it conversation is not easy between the two friends? Why is there no laughter? Why does no lively word fly from the tongue of the perplexed newcomer, who at other times may be very fond of laughter, lively words, conversation about the fair sex, and other cheerful subjects? And why does this friend, probably a new friend and on his first visit–for there will hardly be a second, and the friend will never come again–why is the friend himself so confused, so tongue-tied, in spite of his wit (if he has any), as he looks at the downcast face of his host, who in his turn becomes utterly helpless and at his wits' end after gigantic but fruitless efforts to smooth things over and enliven the conversation, to show his knowledge of polite society, to talk, too, of the fair sex, and by such humble endeavour, to please the poor man, who like a fish out of water has mistakenly come to visit him? Why does the gentleman, all at once remembering some very necessary business which never existed, suddenly seize his hat and hurriedly make off, snatching away his hand from the warm grip of his host, who was trying his utmost to show his regret and retrieve the lost position? Why does the friend chuckle as he goes out of the door, and swear never to come and see this queer creature again, though the queer creature is really a very good fellow, and at the same time he cannot refuse his imagination the little diversion of comparing the queer fellow's countenance during their conversation with the expression of an unhappy kitten treacherously captured, roughly handled, frightened and subjected to all sorts of indignities by children, till, utterly crestfallen, it hides away from them under a chair in the dark, and there must needs at its leisure bristle up, spit, and wash its insulted face with both paws, and long afterwards look angrily at life and nature, and even at the bits saved from the master's dinner for it by the sympathetic housekeeper?"

"Listen," interrupted Nastenka, who had listened to me all the time in amazement, opening her eyes and her little mouth. "Listen; I don't know in the least why it happened and why you ask me such absurd questions; all I know is, that this adventure must have happened word for word to you."

"Doubtless," I answered, with the gravest face.

"Well, since there is no doubt about it, go on," said Nastenka, "because I want very much to know how it will end."

"You want to know, Nastenka, what our hero, that is I–for the hero of the whole business was my humble self-did in his corner? You want to know why I lost my head and was upset for the whole day by the unexpected visit of a friend? You want to know why I was so startled, why I blushed when the door of my room was opened, why I was not able to entertain my visitor, and why I was crushed under the weight of my own hospitality?"

"Why, yes, yes," answered Nastenka, "that's the point. Listen. You describe it all splendidly, but couldn't you perhaps describe it a little less splendidly? You talk as though you were reading it out of a book."

"Nastenka," I answered in a stern and dignified voice, hardly able to keep from laughing, "dear Nastenka, I know I describe splendidly, but, excuse me, I don't know how else to do it. At this moment, dear Nastenka, at this moment I am like the spirit of King Solomon when, after lying a thousand years under seven seals in his urn, those seven seals were at last taken off. At this moment, Nastenka, when we have met at last after such a long separation for I have known you for ages, Nastenka, because I have been looking for some one for ages, and that is a sign that it was you I was looking for, and it was ordained that we should meet now at this moment a thousand valves have opened in my head, and I must let myself flow in a river of words, or I shall choke. And so I beg you not to interrupt me, Nastenka, but listen humbly and obediently, or I will be silent."

"No, no, no! Not at all. Go on! I won't say a word!"

"I will continue. There is, my friend Nastenka, one hour in my day which I like extremely. That is the hour when almost all business, work and duties are over, and every one is hurrying home to dinner, to lie down, to rest, and on the way all are cogitating on other more cheerful subjects relating to their evenings, their nights, and all the rest of their free time. At that hour our-hero for allow me, Nastenka, to tell my story in the third person, for one feels awfully ashamed to tell it in the first person-and so at that hour our hero, who had his work too, was pacing along after the others. But a strange feeling of pleasure set his pale, rather crumpled-looking face working. He looked not with indifference on the evening glow which was slowly fading on the cold Petersburg sky. When I say he looked, I am lying: he did not look at it, but saw it as it were without realizing, as though tired or preoccupied with some other more interesting subject, so that he could scarcely spare a glance for anything about him. He was pleased because till next day he was released from business irksome to him, and happy as a schoolboy let out from the class-room to his games and mischief. Take a look at him, Nastenka; you will see at once that joyful emotion has already had an effect on his weak nerves and morbidly excited fancy. You see he is thinking of something.... Of dinner, do you imagine? Of the evening? What is he looking at like that? Is it at that gentleman of dignified appearance who is bowing so picturesquely to the lady who rolls by in a carriage drawn by prancing horses? No, Nastenka; what are all those trivialities to him now! He is rich now with his own individual life; he has suddenly become rich, and it is not for nothing that the fading sunset sheds its farewell gleams so gaily before him, and calls forth a swarm of impressions from his warmed heart. Now he hardly notices the road, on which the tiniest details at other times would strike him. Now 'the Goddess of Fancy (if you have read Zhukovsky, dear Nastenka) has already with fantastic hand spun her golden warp and begun weaving upon it patterns of marvellous magic life–and who knows, maybe, her fantastic hand has borne him to the seventh crystal heaven far from the excellent granite pavement on which he was walking his way? Try stopping him now, ask him suddenly where he is standing now, through what streets he is going–he will, probably remember nothing, neither where he is going nor where he is standing now, and flushing with vexation he will certainly tell some lie to save appearances. That is why he starts, almost cries out, and looks round with horror when a respectable old lady stops him politely in the middle of the pavement and asks her way. Frowning with vexation he strides on, scarcely noticing that more than one passer-by smiles and turns round to look after him, and that a little girl, moving out of his way in alarm, laughs aloud, gazing open-eyed at his broad meditative smile and gesticulations. But fancy catches up in its playful flight the old woman, the curious passers-by, and the laughing child, and the peasants spending their nights in their barges on Fontanka (our hero, let us suppose, is walking along the canal-side at that moment), and capriciously weaves every one and everything into the canvas like a fly in a spider's web. And it is only after the queer fellow has returned to his comfortable den with fresh stores for his mind to work on, has sat down and finished his dinner, that he comes to himself, when Matrona who waits upon him-always thoughtful and depressed-clears the table and gives him his pipe; he comes to himself then and recalls with surprise that he has dined, though he has absolutely no notion how it has happened. It has grown dark in the room; his soul is sad and empty; the whole kingdom of fancies drops to pieces about him, drops to pieces without a trace, without a sound, floats away like a dream, and he cannot himself remember what he was dreaming. But a vague sensation faintly stirs his heart and sets it aching, some new desire temptingly tickles and excites his fancy, and imperceptibly evokes a swarm of fresh phantoms. Stillness reigns in the little room; imagination is fostered by solitude and idleness; it is faintly smouldering, faintly simmering, like the water with which old Matrona is making her coffee as she moves quietly about in the kitchen close by. Now it breaks out spasmodically; and the book, picked up aimlessly and at random, drops from my dreamer's hand before he has reached the third page. His imagination is again stirred and at work, and again a new world, a new fascinating life opens vistas before him. A fresh dream–fresh happiness! A fresh rush of delicate, voluptuous poison! What is real life to him! To his corrupted eyes we live, you and I, Nastenka, so torpidly, slowly, insipidly; in his eyes we are all so dissatisfied with our fate, so exhausted by our life! And, truly, see how at first sight everything is cold, morose, as though ill-humoured among us.... Poor things! thinks our dreamer. And it is no wonder that he thinks it! Look at these magic phantasms, which so enchantingly, so whimsically, so carelessly and freely group before him in such a magic, animated picture, in which the most prominent figure in the foreground is of course himself, our dreamer, in his precious person. See what varied adventures, what an endless swarm of ecstatic dreams. You ask, perhaps, what he is dreaming of. Why ask that?–why, of everything... of the lot of the poet, first unrecognized, then crowned with laurels; of friendship with Hoffmann, St. Bartholomew's Night, of Diana Vernon, of playing the hero at the taking of Kazan by Ivan

Vassilyevitch, of Clara Mowbray, of Effie Deans, of the council of the prelates and Huss before them, of the rising of the dead in 'Robert the Devil' (do you remember the music, it smells of the churchyard!), of Minna and Brenda, of the battle of Berezina, of the reading of a poem at Countess V. D.'s, of Danton, of Cleopatra ei suoi amanti, of a little house in Kolomna, of a little home of one's own and beside one a dear creature who listens to one on a winter's evening, opening her little mouth and eyes as you are listening to me now, my angel.... No, Nastenka, what is there, what is there for him, voluptuous sluggard, in this life, for which you and I have such a longing? He thinks that this is a poor pitiful life, not foreseeing that for him too, maybe, sometime the mournful hour may strike, when for one day of that pitiful life he would give all his years of phantasy, and would give them not only for joy and for happiness, but without caring to make distinctions in that hour of sadness, remorse and unchecked grief. But so far that threatening has not arrived–he desires nothing, because he is superior to all desire, because he has everything, because he is satiated, because he is the artist of his own life, and creates it for himself every hour to suit his latest whim. And you know this fantastic world of fairyland is so easily, so naturally created! As though it were not a delusion! Indeed, he is ready to believe at some moments that all this life is not suggested by feeling, is not mirage, not a delusion of the imagination, but that it is concrete, real, substantial! Why is it, Nastenka, why is it at such moments one holds one's breath? Why, by what sorcery, through what incomprehensible caprice, is the pulse quickened, does a tear start from the dreamer's eye, while his pale moist cheeks glow, while his whole being is suffused with an inexpressible sense of consolation? Why is it that whole sleepless nights pass like a flash in inexhaustible gladness and happiness, and when the dawn gleams rosy at the window and daybreak floods the gloomy room with uncertain, fantastic light, as in Petersburg, our dreamer, worn out and exhausted, flings himself on his bed and drops asleep with thrills of delight in his morbidly overwrought spirit, and with a weary sweet ache in his heart? Yes, Nastenka, one deceives oneself and unconsciously believes that real true passion is stirring one's soul; one unconsciously believes that there is something living, tangible in one's immaterial dreams! And is it delusion? Here love, for instance, is bound up with all its fathomless joy, all its torturing agonies in his bosom.... Only look at him, and you will be convinced! Would you believe, looking at him, dear Nastenka, that he has never known her whom he loves in his ecstatic dreams? Can it be that he has only seen her in seductive visions, and that this passion has been nothing but a dream? Surely they must have spent years hand in hand together–alone the two of them, casting off all the world and each uniting his or her life with the other's? Surely when the hour of parting came she must have lain sobbing and grieving on his bosom, heedless of the tempest raging under the sullen sky, heedless of the wind which snatches and bears away the tears from her black eyelashes? Can all of that have been a dream–and that garden, dejected, forsaken, run wild, with its little moss-grown paths, solitary, gloomy, where they used to walk so happily together, where they hoped, grieved, loved, loved each other so long, "so long and so fondly?" And that queer ancestral house where she spent so many years lonely and sad with her morose old husband, always silent and splenetic, who frightened them, while timid as children they hid their love from each other? What torments they suffered, what agonies of terror, how innocent, how pure was their love, and how (I need hardly say, Nastenka) malicious people were! And, good Heavens! surely he met her afterwards, far from their native shores, under alien skies, in the hot south in the divinely eternal city, in the dazzling splendour of the ball to the crash of music, in a palazzo (it must be in a palazzo), drowned in a sea of lights, on the balcony, wreathed in myrtle and roses, where, recognizing him, she hurriedly removes her mask and whispering, 'I am free,' flings herself trembling into his arms, and with a cry of rapture, clinging to one another, in one instant they forget their sorrow and their parting and all their agonies, and the gloomy house and the old man and the dismal garden in that distant land, and the seat on which with a last passionate kiss she tore herself away from his arms numb with anguish and despair.... Oh, Nastenka, you must admit that one would start, betray confusion, and blush like a schoolboy who has just stuffed in his pocket an apple stolen from a neighbour's garden, when your uninvited visitor, some stalwart, lanky fellow, a festive soul fond of a joke, opens your door and shouts out as though nothing were happening: 'My dear boy, I have this minute come from Pavlovsk.' My goodness! the old count is dead, unutterable happiness is close at hand–and people arrive from Pavlovsk!"

Finishing my pathetic appeal, I paused pathetically. I remembered that I had an intense desire to force myself to laugh, for I was already feeling that a malignant demon was stirring within me, that there was a lump in my throat, that my chin was beginning to twitch, and that my eyes were growing more and more moist.

I expected Nastenka, who listened to me opening her clever eyes, would break into her childish, irrepressible laugh; and I was already regretting that I had gone so far, that I had unnecessarily described what had long been simmering in my heart, about which I could speak as though from a written account of it, because I had long ago passed judgment on myself and now could not resist reading it, making my confession, without expecting to be understood; but to my surprise she was silent, waiting a little, then she faintly pressed my hand and with timid sympathy asked–

"Surely you haven't lived like that all your life?"

"All my life, Nastenka," I answered; "all my life, and it seems to me I shall go on so to the end."

"No, that won't do," she said uneasily, "that must not be; and so, maybe, I shall spend all my life beside grandmother. Do you know, it is not at all good to live like that?"

"I know, Nastenka, I know!" I cried, unable to restrain my feelings longer. "And I realize now, more than ever, that I have lost all my best years! And now I know it and feel it more painfully from recognizing that God has sent me you, my good angel, to tell me that and show it. Now that I sit beside you and talk to you it is strange for me to think of the future, for in the future–there is loneliness again, again this musty, useless life; and what shall I have to dream of when I have been so happy in reality beside you! Oh, may you be blessed, dear girl, for not having repulsed me at first, for enabling me to say that for two evenings, at least, I have lived."

"Oh, no, no!" cried Nastenka and tears glistened in her eyes. "No, it mustn't be so any more; we must not part like that! what are two evenings?"

"Oh, Nastenka, Nastenkal Do you know how far you have reconciled me to myself? Do you know now that I shall not think so ill of myself, as I have at some moments? Do you know that, maybe, I shall leave off grieving over the crime and sin of my life? for such a life is a crime and a sin. And do not imagine that I have been exaggerating anything–for goodness' sake don't think that, Nastenka: for at times such misery comes over me, such misery.... Because it begins to seem to me at such times that I am incapable of beginning a life in real life, because it has seemed to me that I have lost all touch, all instinct for the actual, the real; because at last I have cursed myself; because after my fantastic nights I have moments of returning sobriety, which are awful! Meanwhile, you hear the whirl and roar of the crowd in the vortex of life around you; you hear, you see, men living in reality; you see that life for them is not forbidden, that their life does not float away like a dream, like a vision; that their life is being eternally renewed, eternally youthful, and not one hour of it is the same as another; while fancy is so spiritless, monotonous to vulgarity and easily scared, the slave of shadows, of the idea, the slave of the first cloud that shrouds the sun, and overcasts with depression the true Petersburg heart so devoted to the sun–and what is fancy in depression! One feels that this inexhaustible fancy is weary at last and worn out with continual exercise, because one is growing into manhood, outgrowing one's old ideals: they are being shattered into fragments, into dust; if there is no other life one must build one up from the fragments. And meanwhile the soul longs and craves for something else! And in vain the dreamer rakes over his old dreams, as though seeking a spark among the embers, to fan them into flame, to warm his chilled heart by the rekindled fire, and to rouse up in it again all that was so sweet, that touched his heart, that set his blood boiling, drew tears from his eyes, and so luxuriously deceived him! Do you know, Nastenka, the point I have reached? Do you know that I am forced now to celebrate the anniversary of my own sensations, the anniversary of that which was once so sweet, which never existed in reality–for this anniversary is kept in memory of those same foolish, shadowy dreams–and to do this because those foolish dreams are no more, because I have nothing to earn them with; you know even dreams do not come for nothing! Do you know that I love now to recall and visit at certain dates the places where I was once happy in my own way? I love to build up my present in harmony with the irrevocable past, and I often wander like a shadow, aimless, sad and dejected, about the streets and crooked lanes of Petersburg. What memories they are! To remember, for instance, that here just a year ago, just at this time, at this hour, on this pavement, I wandered just as lonely, just as dejected as to-day. And one remembers that then one's dreams were sad, and though the past was no better one feels as though it had somehow been better, and that life was more peaceful, that one was free from the black thoughts that haunt one now; that one was free from the gnawing of conscience–the gloomy, sullen gnawing which now gives me no rest by day or by night. And one asks oneself where are one's dreams. And one shakes one's head and says how rapidly the years fly by! And again one asks oneself what has one done with one's years. Where have you buried your best days? Have you lived or not? Look, one says to oneself, look how cold the world is growing. Some more years will pass, and after them will come gloomy solitude; then will come old age trembling on its crutch, and after it misery and desolation. Your fantastic world will grow pale, your dreams will fade and die and will fall like the yellow leaves from the trees.... Oh, Nastenka! you know it will be sad to be left alone, utterly alone, and to have not even anything to regret–nothing, absolutely nothing... for all that you have lost, all that, all was nothing, stupid, simple nullity, there has been nothing but dreams!"

"Come, don't work on my feelings any more," said Nastenka, wiping away a tear which was trickling down her cheek. "Now it's over! Now we shall be two together. Now, whatever happens to me, we will never part. Listen; I am a simple girl, I have not had much education, though grandmother did get a teacher for me, but truly I understand you, for all that you have described I have been through myself, when grandmother pinned me to her dress. Of course, I should not have described it so well as you have; I am not educated," she added timidly, for she was still feeling a sort of respect for my pathetic eloquence and lofty style; "but I am very glad that you have been quite open with me. Now I know you thoroughly, all of you. And do you know what? I want to tell you my history too, all without concealment, and after that you must give me advice. You are a very clever man; will you promise to give me advice?"

"Ah, Nastenka," I cried, "though I have never given advice, still less sensible advice, yet I see now that if we always go on like this that it will be very sensible, and that each of us will give the other a great deal of sensible advice! Well, my pretty Nastenka, what sort of advice do you want? Tell me frankly; at this moment I am so gay and happy, so bold and sensible, that it won't be difficult for me to find words."

"No, no!" Nastenka interrupted, laughing. "I don't only want sensible advice, I want warm brotherly advice, as though you had been fond of me all your life!"

"Agreed, Nastenka, agreed!" I cried delighted; "and if I had been fond of you for twenty years, I couldn't have been fonder of you than I am now."

"Your hand," said Nastenka.

"Here it is," said I, giving her my hand.

"And so let us begin my history!"

Nastenka's History

Half my story you know already–that is, you know that I have an old grandmother...." "If the other half is as brief as that..." I interrupted, laughing.

"Be quiet and listen. First of all you must agree not to interrupt me, or else, perhaps I shall get in a muddle! Come, listen quietly.

"I have an old grandmother. I came into her hands when I was quite a little girl, for my father and mother are dead. It must be supposed that grandmother was once richer, for now she recalls better days. She taught me French, and then got a teacher for me. When I was fifteen (and now I am seventeen) we gave up having lessons. It was at that time that I got into mischief; what I did I won't tell you; it's enough to say that it wasn't very important. But grandmother called me to her one morning and said that as she was blind she could not look after me; she took a pin and pinned my dress to hers, and said that we should sit like that for the rest of our lives if, of course, I did not become a better girl. In fact, at first it was impossible to get away from her: I had to work, to read and to study all beside grandmother. I tried to deceive her once, and persuaded Fekla to sit in my place. Fekla is our charwoman, she is deaf. Fekla sat there instead of me; grandmother was asleep in her armchair at the time, and I went off to see a friend close by. Well, it ended in trouble. Grandmother woke up while I was out, and

"No, no!" Nastenka interrupted, laughing. "I don't only want sensible advice, I want warm brotherly advice, as though you had been fond of me all your life!"

"Agreed, Nastenka, agreed!" I cried delighted; "and if I had been fond of you for twenty years, I couldn't have been fonder of you than I am now."

"Your hand," said Nastenka.

"Here it is," said I, giving her my hand.

"And so let us begin my history!"

Nastenka's History

"Half my story you know already–that is, you know that I have an old grandmother...." "If the other half is as brief as that..." I interrupted, laughing.

"Be quiet and listen. First of all you must agree not to interrupt me, or else, perhaps I shall get in a muddle! Come, listen quietly.

"I have an old grandmother. I came into her hands when I was quite a little girl, for my father and mother are dead. It must be supposed that grandmother was once richer, for now she recalls better days. She taught me French, and then got a teacher for me. When I was fifteen (and now I am seventeen) we gave up having lessons. It was at that time that I got into mischief; what I did I won't tell you; it's enough to say that it wasn't very important. But grandmother called me to her one morning and said that as she was blind she could not look after me; she took a pin and pinned my dress to hers, and said that we should sit like that for the rest of our lives if, of course, I did not become a better girl. In fact, at first it was impossible to get away from her: I had to work, to read and to study all beside grandmother. I tried to deceive her once, and persuaded Fekla to sit in my place. Fekla is our charwoman, she is deaf. Fekla sat there instead of me; grandmother was asleep in her armchair at the time, and I went off to see a friend close by. Well, it ended in trouble. Grandmother woke up while I was out, and asked some questions; she thought I was still sitting quietly in my place. Fekla saw that grandmother was asking her something, but could not tell what it was; she wondered what to do, undid the pin and ran away...."

At this point Nastenka stopped and began laughing. I laughed with her. She left off at once.

"I tell you what, don't you laugh at grandmother. I laugh because it's funny.... What can I do, since grandmother is like that; but yet I am fond of her in a way. Oh, well, I did catch it that time. I had to sit down in my place at once, and after that I was not allowed to stir.

"Oh, I forgot to tell you that our house belongs to us, that is to grandmother; it is a little wooden house with three windows as old as grandmother herself, with a little upper storey; well, there moved into our upper storey a new lodger."

"Then you had an old lodger," I observed casually.

"Yes, of course," answered Nastenka, "and one who knew how to hold his tongue better than you do. In fact, he hardly ever used his tongue at all. He was a dumb, blind, lame, dried-up little old man, so that at last he could not go on living, he died; so then we had to find a new lodger, for we could not live without a lodger–the rent, together with grandmother's pension, is almost all we have. But the new lodger, as luck would have it, was a young man, a stranger not of these parts. As he did not haggle over the rent, grandmother accepted him, and only afterwards she asked me: 'Tell me, Nastenka, what is our lodger like–is he young or old?' I did not want to lie, so I told grandmother that he wasn't exactly young and that he wasn't old.

"'And is he pleasant looking?' asked grandmother.

"Again I did not want to tell a lie: 'Yes, he is pleasant looking, grandmother,' I said. And grandmother said: 'Oh, what a nuisance, what a nuisance! I tell you this, grandchild, that you may not be looking after him. What times these are! Why a paltry lodger like this, and he must be pleasant looking too; it was very different in the old days!'"

"Grandmother was always regretting the old days–she was younger in old days, and the sun was warmer in old days, and cream did not turn so sour in old days–it was always the old days! I would sit still and hold my tongue and think to myself: why did grandmother suggest it to me? Why did she ask whether the lodger was young and good-looking? But that was all, I just thought it, began counting my stitches again, went on knitting my stocking, and forgot all about it.

"Well, one morning the lodger came in to see us; he asked about a promise to paper his rooms. One thing led to another. Grandmother was talkative, and she said: 'Go, Nastenka, into my bedroom and bring me my reckoner.' I jumped up at once; I blushed all over, I don't know why, and forgot I was sitting pinned to grandmother; instead of quietly undoing the pin, so that the lodger should not see–I jumped so that grandmother's chair moved. When I saw that the lodger knew all about me now, I blushed, stood still as though I had been shot, and suddenly began to cry–I felt so ashamed and miserable at that minute, that I didn't know where to look! Grandmother called out, 'What are you waiting for? and I went on worse than ever. When the lodger saw, saw that I was ashamed on his account, he bowed and went away at once!

"After that I felt ready to die at the least sound in the passage. 'It's the lodger, I kept thinking; I stealthily undid the pin in case. But it always turned out not to be, he never came. A fortnight passed; the lodger sent word through Fyokla that he had a great number of French books, and that they were all good books that I might read, so would not grandmother like me to read them that I might not be dull? Grandmother agreed with gratitude, but kept asking if they were moral books, for if the books were immoral it would be out of the question, one would learn evil from them."

"'And what should I learn, grandmother? What is there written in them?'

"'Ah,' she said, 'what's described in them, is how young men seduce virtuous girls; how, on the excuse that they want to marry them, they carry them off from their parents' houses; how afterwards they leave these unhappy girls to their fate, and they perish in the most pitiful way. I read a great many books,' said grandmother, 'and it is all so well described that one sits up all night and reads them on the sly. So mind you don't read them, Nastenka,' said she. 'What books has he sent?

"'They are all Walter Scott's novels, grandmother.'

"'Walter Scott's novels! But stay, isn't there some trick about it? Look, hasn't he stuck a love-letter among them?'

"'No, grandmother,' I said, 'there isn't a love-letter.'

"'But look under the binding; they sometimes stuff it under the bindings, the rascals!'

"'No, grandmother, there is nothing under the binding.'

"'Well, that's all right.'

"So we began reading Walter Scott, and in a month or so we had read almost half. Then he sent us more and more. He sent us Pushkin, too; so that at last I could not get on without a book and left off dreaming of how fine it would be to marry a Chinese Prince.

"That's how things were when I chanced one day to meet our lodger on the stairs. Grandmother had sent me to fetch something. He stopped, I blushed and he blushed; he laughed, though, said good-morning to me, asked after grandmother, and said, 'Well, have you read the books?' I answered that I had. 'Which did you like best?' he asked. I said, 'Ivanhoe, and Pushkin best of all,' and so our talk ended for that time.

"A week later I met him again on the stairs. That time grandmother had not sent me, I wanted to get something for myself. It was past two, and the lodger used to come home at that time. 'Good-afternoon,' said he. I said good-afternoon, too.

"'Aren't you dull,' he said, 'sitting all day with your grandmother?'

"When he asked that, I blushed, I don't know why; I felt ashamed, and again I felt offended–I suppose because other people had begun to ask me about that. I wanted to go away without answering, but I hadn't the strength.

"'Listen,' he said, 'you are a good girl. Excuse my speaking to you like that, but I assure you that I wish for your welfare quite as much as your grandmother. Have you no friends that you could go and visit?'

"I told him I hadn't any, that I had had no friend but Mashenka, and she had gone away to Pskov.

"'Listen,' he said, 'would you like to go to the theatre with me?'

"'To the theatre. What about grandmother?'

"'But you must go without your grandmother's knowing it,' he said.

"'No,' I said, 'I don't want to deceive grandmother. Good-bye.

"'Well, good-bye,' he answered, and said nothing more.

"Only after dinner he came to see us; sat a long time talking to grandmother; asked her whether she ever went out anywhere, whether she had acquaintances, and suddenly said: 'I have taken a box at the opera for this evening; they are giving The Barber of Seville. My friends meant to go, but afterwards refused, so the ticket is left on my hands.' 'The Barber of Seville,' cried grandmother; 'why, the same they used to act in old days?'

"'Yes, it's the same barber,' he said, and glanced at me. I saw what it meant and turned crimson, and my heart began throbbing with suspense.

"'To be sure, I know it,' said grandmother; 'why, I took the part of Rosina myself in old days, at a private performance!'

"'So wouldn't you like to go to-day?' said the lodger. 'Or my ticket will be wasted.'

"'By all means let us go,' said grandmother; why shouldn't we? And my Nastenka here has never been to the theatre.'

"My goodness, what joy! We got ready at once, put on our best clothes, and set off. Though grandmother was blind, still she wanted to hear the music; besides, she is a kind old soul, what she cared most for was to amuse me, we should never have gone of ourselves.

"What my impressions of The Barber of Seville were I won't tell you; but all that evening our lodger looked at me so nicely, talked so nicely, that I saw at once that he had meant to test me in the morning when he proposed that I should go with him alone. Well, it was joy! I went to bed so proud, so gay, my heart beat so that I was a little feverish, and all night I was raving about The Barber of Seville.

"I expected that he would come and see us more and more often after that, but it wasn't so at all. He almost entirely gave up coming. He would just come in about once a month, and then only to invite us to the theatre. We went twice again. Only I wasn't at all pleased with that; I saw that he was simply sorry for me because I was so hardly treated by grandmother, and that was all. As time went on, I grew more and more restless, I couldn't sit still, I couldn't read, I couldn't work; sometimes I laughed and did something to annoy grandmother, at another time I would cry. At last I grew thin and was very nearly ill. The opera season was over, and our lodger had quite given up coming to see us; whenever we met–always on the same staircase, of course–he would bow so silently, so gravely, as though he did not want to speak, and go down to the front door, while I went on standing in the middle of the stairs, as red as a cherry, for all the blood rushed to my head at the sight of him.

"Now the end is near. Just a year ago, in May, the lodger came to us and said to grandmother that he had finished his business here, and that he must go back to Moscow for a year. When I heard that, I sank into a chair half dead; grandmother did not notice anything; and having informed us that he should be leaving us, he bowed and went away.

"What was I to do? I thought and thought and fretted and fretted, and at last I made up my mind. Next day he was to go away, and I made up my mind to end it all that evening when grandmother went to bed. And so it happened. I made up all my clothes in a parcel–all the linen I needed–and with the parcel in my hand, more dead than alive, went upstairs to our lodger. I believe I must have stayed an hour on the staircase. When I opened his door he cried out as he looked at me. He thought I was a ghost, and rushed to give me some water, for I could hardly stand up. My heart beat so violently that my head ached, and I did not know what I was doing. When I recovered I began by laying my parcel on his bed, sat down beside it, hid my face in my hands and went into floods of tears. I think he understood it all at once, and looked at me so sadly that my heart was torn.

"'Listen,' he began, 'listen, Nastenka, I can't do anything; I am a poor man, for I have nothing, not even a decent berth. How could we live, if I were to marry you?'

"We talked a long time; but at last I got quite frantic, I said I could not go on living with grandmother, that I should run away from her, that I did not want to be pinned to her, and that I would go to Moscow if he liked, because I could not live without him. Shame and pride and love were all clamouring in me at once, and I fell on the bed almost in convulsions, I was so afraid of a refusal.

"He sat for some minutes in silence, then got up, came up to me and took me by the hand.

"'Listen, my dear good Nastenka, listen; I swear to you that if I am ever in a position to marry, you shall make my happiness. I assure you that now you are the only one who could make me happy. Listen, I am going to Moscow and shall be there just a year; I hope to establish my position. When I come back, if you still love me, I swear that we will be happy. Now it is impossible, I am not able, I have not the right to promise anything. Well, I repeat, if it is not within a year it will certainly be some time; that is, of course, if you do not prefer any one else, for I cannot and dare not bind you by any sort of promise.'

"That was what he said to me, and next day he went away. We agreed together not to say a word to grandmother: that was his wish. Well, my history is nearly finished now. Just a year has past. He has arrived; he has been here three days, and, and

"And what?" I cried, impatient to hear the end.

"And up to now has not shown himself!" answered Nastenka, as though screwing up all her courage. "There's no sign or sound of him."

Here she stopped, paused for a minute, bent her head, and covering her face with her hands broke into such sobs that it sent a pang to my heart to hear them. I had not in the least expected such a dénouement.

"Nastenka," I began timidly in an ingratiating voice, "Nastenka! For goodness' sake don't cry! How do you know? Perhaps he is not here yet...."

"He is, he is," Nastenka repeated. "He is here, and I know it. We made an agreement at the time, that evening. before he went away: when we said all that I have told you, and had come to an understanding, then we came out here for a walk on this embankment. It was ten o'clock; we sat on this seat. I was not crying then; it was sweet to me to hear what he said.... And he said that he would come to us directly he arrived, and if I did not refuse him, then we would tell grandmother about it all. Now he is here, I know it, and yet he does not come!"

And again she burst into tears.

"Good God, can I do nothing to help you in your sorrow?" I cried jumping up from the seat in utter despair. "Tell me, Nastenka, wouldn't it be possible for me to go to him?"

"Would that be possible?" she asked suddenly, raising her head.

"No, of course not," I said pulling myself up; "but I tell you what, write a letter."

"No, that's impossible, I can't do that," she answered with decision, bending her head and not looking at me.

"How impossible–why is it impossible?" I went on, clinging to my idea. "But, Nastenka, it depends what sort of letter; there are letters and letters and..... Ah, Nastenka, I am right; trust to me, trust to me, I will not give you bad advice. It can all be arranged! You took the first step–why not now?"

"I can't. I can't! It would seem as though I were forcing myself on him...."

"Ah, my good little Nastenka," I said, hardly able to conceal a smile; "no, no, you have a right to, in fact, because he made you a promise. Besides, I can see from everything that he is a man of delicate feeling; that he behaved very well," I went on, more and more carried away by the logic of my own arguments and convictions. "How did he behave? He bound himself by a promise: he said that if he married at all he would marry no one but you; he gave you full liberty to refuse him at once.... Under such circumstances you may take the first step; you have the right; you are in the privileged position-if, for instance, you wanted to free him from his promise...."

"Listen; how would you write?"

"Write what?"

"This letter."

"I tell you how I would write: 'Dear Sir.'..."

"Must I really begin like that, 'Dear Sir'?"

"You certainly must! Though, after all, I don't know, I imagine...."

"Well, well, what next?"

""Dear Sir,–I must apologize for—' But, no, there's no need to apologize; the fact itself justifies everything. Write simply:–

"'I am writing to you. Forgive me my impatience; but I have been happy for a whole year in hope; am I to blame for being unable to endure a day of doubt now? Now that you have come, perhaps you have changed your mind. If so, this letter is to tell you that I do not repine, nor blame you. I do not blame you because I have no power over your heart, such is my fate!

"'You are an honourable man. You will not smile or be vexed at these impatient lines. Remember they are written by a poor girl; that she is alone; that she has no one to direct her, no one to advise her, and that she herself could never control her heart. But forgive me that a doubt has stolen–if only for one instant–into my heart. You are not capable of insulting, even in thought, her who so loved and so loves you."

"Yes, yes; that's exactly what I was thinking!" cried Nastenka, and her eyes beamed with delight. "Oh, you have solved my difficulties: God has sent you to me! Thank you, thank you!"

"What for? What for? For God's sending me?" I answered, looking delighted at her joyful little face.

"Why, yes; for that too."

"Ah, Nastenka! Why, one thanks some people for being alive at the same time with one; I thank you for having met me, for my being able to remember you all my life!"

"Well, enough, enough! But now I tell you what, listen: we made an agreement then that as soon as he arrived he would let me know, by leaving a letter with some good simple people of my acquaintance who know nothing about it; or, if it were impossible to write a letter to me, for a letter does not always tell everything, he would be here at ten o'clock on the day he arrived, where we had arranged to meet. I know he has arrived already; but now it's the third day, and there's no sign of him and no letter. It's impossible for me to get away from grandmother in the morning. Give my letter to-morrow to those kind people I spoke to you about: they will send it on to him, and if there is an answer you bring it to-morrow at ten o'clock."

"But the letter, the letter! You see, you must write the letter first! So perhaps it must all be the day after to-morrow."

"The letter..." said Nastenka, a little confused, "the letter... but...."

But she did not finish. At first she turned her little face away from me, flushed like a rose, and suddenly I felt in my hand a letter which had evidently been written long before, all ready and sealed up. A familiar sweet and charming reminiscence floated through my mind.

"R, o–Ro; s, i–si; n, a–na," I began.

"Rosina!" we both hummed together; I almost embracing her with delight, while she blushed as only she could blush, and laughed through the tears which gleamed like pearls on her black eyelashes.

"Come, enough, enough! Good-bye now," she said speaking rapidly. "Here is the letter, here is the address to which you are to take it. Good-bye, till we meet again! Till to-morrow!"

She pressed both my hands warmly, nodded her head, and flew like an arrow down her side street. I stood still for a long time following her with my eyes.

"Till to-morrow! till to-morrow!" was ringing in my ears as she vanished from my sight.

Third Night

To-day was a gloomy, rainy day without a glimmer of sunlight, like the old age before me. I am oppressed by such strange thoughts, such gloomy sensations; questions still so obscure to me are crowding into my brain– and I seem to have neither power nor will to settle them. It's not for me to settle all this!

To-day we shall not meet. Yesterday, when we said good-bye, the clouds began gathering over the sky and a mist rose. I said that to-morrow it would be a bad day; she made no answer, she did not want to speak against her wishes; for her that day was bright and clear, not one cloud should obscure her happiness.

"If it rains we shall not see each other," she said, "I shall not come."

I thought that she would not notice to-day's rain, and yet she has not come.

Yesterday was our third interview, our third white night....

But how fine joy and happiness makes any one! How brimming over with love the heart is! One seems longing to pour out one's whole heart; one wants everything to be gay, everything to be laughing. And how infectious that joy is! There was such a softness in her words, such a kindly feeling in her heart towards me yesterday.... How solicitous and friendly she was; how tenderly she tried to give me courage! Oh, the coquetry of happiness! While I... I took it all for the genuine thing, I thought that she....

But, my God, how could I have thought it? How could I have been so blind, when everything had been taken by another already, when nothing was mine; when, in fact, her very tenderness to me, her anxiety, her love... yes, love for me, was nothing else but joy at the thought of seeing another man so soon, desire to include me, too, in her happiness?... When he did not come, when we waited in vain, she frowned, she grew timid and discouraged. Her movements, her words, were no longer so light, so playful, so gay; and, strange to say, she redoubled her attentiveness to me, as though instinctively desiring to lavish on me what she desired for herself so anxiously, if her wishes were not accomplished. My Nastenka was so downcast, so dismayed, that I think she realized at last that I loved her, and was sorry for my poor love. So when we are unhappy we feel the unhappiness of others more; feeling is not destroyed but concentrated....

I went to meet her with a full heart, and was all impatience. I had no presentiment that I should feel as I do now, that it would not all end happily. She was beaming with pleasure; she was expecting an answer. The answer was himself. He was to come, to run at her call. She arrived a whole hour before I did. At first she giggled at everything, laughed at every word I said. I began talking, but relapsed into silence.

"Do you know why I am so glad," she said, "so glad to look at you?– why I like you so much to-day?"

"Well?" I asked, and my heart began throbbing.

"I like you because you have not fallen in love with me. You know that some men in your place would have been pestering and worrying me, would have been sighing and miserable, while you are so nice!"

Then she wrung my hand so hard that I almost cried out. She laughed.

"Goodness, what a friend you are!" she began gravely a minute later. "God sent you to me. What would have happened to me if you had not been with me now? How disinterested you are! How truly you care for me! When I am married we will be great friends, more than brother and sister; I shall care almost as I do for him...."

I felt horribly sad at that moment, yet something like laughter was stirring in my soul.

"You are very much upset," I said; "you are frightened; you think he won't come."

"Oh dear!" she answered; "if I were less happy, I believe I should cry at your lack of faith, at your reproaches. However, you have made me think and have given me a lot to think about; but I shall think later, and now I will own that you are right. Yes, I am somehow not myself; I am all suspense, and feel everything as it were too lightly. But hush! that's enough about feelings...."

At that moment we heard footsteps, and in the darkness we saw a figure coming towards us. We both started; she almost cried out; I dropped her hand and made a movement as though to walk away. But we were mistaken, it was not he.

"What are you afraid of? Why did you let go of my hand?" she said, giving it to me again. "Come, what is it? We will meet him together; I want him to see how fond we are of each other."

"How fond we are of each other!" I cried. ("Oh, Nastenka, Nastenka," I thought, "how much you have told me in that saying! Such fondness at certain moments makes the heart cold and the soul heavy. Your hand is cold, mine burns like fire. How blind you are, Nastenka!... Oh, how unbearable a happy person is sometimes! But I could not be angry with you!")

At last my heart was too full.

"Listen, Nastenka!" I cried. "Do you know how it has been with me all day."

"Why, how, how? Tell me quickly! Why have you said nothing all this time?"

"To begin with, Nastenka, when I had carried out all your commissions, given the letter, gone to see your good friends, then... then I went home and went to bed."

"Is that all?" she interrupted, laughing.

"Yes, almost all," I answered restraining myself, for foolish tears were already starting into my eyes. "I woke an hour before our appointment, and yet, as it were, I had not been asleep. I don't know what happened to me. I came to tell you all about it, feeling as though time were standing still, feeling as though one sensation, one feeling must remain with me from that time for ever; feeling as though one minute must go on for all eternity, and as though all life had come to a standstill for me.... When I woke up it seemed as though some musical motive long familiar, heard somewhere in the past, forgotten and voluptuously sweet, had come back to me now. It seemed to me that it had been clamouring at my heart all my life, and only now...."

"Oh my goodness, my goodness," Nastenka interrupted, "what does all that mean? I don't understand a word."

"Ah, Nastenka, I wanted somehow to convey to you that strange impression...." I began in a plaintive voice, in which there still lay hid a hope, though a very faint one.

"Leave off. Hush!" she said, and in one instant the sly puss had guessed.

Suddenly she became extraordinarily talkative, gay, mischievous; she took my arm, laughed, wanted me to laugh too, and every confused word I uttered evoked from her prolonged ringing laughter.... I began to feel angry, she had suddenly begun flirting.

"Do you know," she began, "I feel a little vexed that you are not in love with me? There's no understanding human nature! But all the same, Mr. Unapproachable, you cannot blame me for being so simple; I tell you everything, everything, whatever foolish thought comes into my head."

"Listen! That's eleven, I believe," I said as the slow chime of a bell rang out from a distant tower. She suddenly stopped, left off laughing and began to count.

"Yes, it's eleven," she said at last in a timid, uncertain voice.

I regretted at once that I had frightened her, making her count the strokes, and I cursed myself for my spiteful impulse; I felt sorry for her, and did not know how to atone for what I had done.

I began comforting her, seeking for reasons for his not coming, advancing various arguments, proofs. No one could have been easier to deceive than she was at that moment; and, indeed, any one at such a moment listens gladly to any consolation, whatever it may be, and is overjoyed if a shadow of excuse can be found.

"And indeed it's an absurd thing," I began, warming to my task and admiring the extraordinary clearness of my argument, "why, he could not have come; you have muddled and confused me, Nastenka, so that I too, have lost count of the time.... Only think: he can scarcely have received the letter; suppose he is not able to come, suppose he is going to answer the letter, could not come before to-morrow. I will go for it as soon as it's light to-morrow and let you know at once. Consider, there are thousands of possibilities; perhaps he was not at home when the letter came, and may not have read it even now! Anything may happen, you know."

"Yes, yes!" said Nastenka. "I did not think of that. Of course anything may happen?" she went on in a tone that offered no opposition, though some other far-away thought could be heard like a vexatious discord in it. "I tell you what you must do," she said, "you go as early as possible to-morrow morning, and if you get anything let me know at once. You know where I live, don't you?"

And she began repeating her address to me.

Then she suddenly became so tender, so solicitous with me. She seemed to listen attentively to what I told her; but when I asked her some question she was silent, was confused, and turned her head away. I looked into her eyes–yes, she was crying.

"How can you? How can you? Oh, what a baby you are! what childishness!... Come, come!"

"Oh my goodness, my goodness," Nastenka interrupted, "what does all that mean? I don't understand a word."

"Ah, Nastenka, I wanted somehow to convey to you that strange impression...." I began in a plaintive voice, in which there still lay hid a hope, though a very faint one.

"Leave off. Hush!" she said, and in one instant the sly puss had guessed.

Suddenly she became extraordinarily talkative, gay, mischievous; she took my arm, laughed, wanted me to laugh too, and every confused word I uttered evoked from her prolonged ringing laughter.... I began to feel angry, she had suddenly begun flirting.

"Do you know," she began, "I feel a little vexed that you are not in love with me? There's no understanding human nature! But all the same, Mr. Unapproachable, you cannot blame me for being so simple; I tell you everything, everything, whatever foolish thought comes into my head."

"Listen! That's eleven, I believe," I said as the slow chime of a bell rang out from a distant tower. She suddenly stopped, left off laughing and began to count.

"Yes, it's eleven," she said at last in a timid, uncertain voice.

I regretted at once that I had frightened her, making her count the strokes, and I cursed myself for my spiteful impulse; I felt sorry for her, and did not know how to atone for what I had done.

I began comforting her, seeking for reasons for his not coming, advancing various arguments, proofs. Noone could have been easier to deceive than she was at that moment; and, indeed, any one at such a moment listens gladly to any consolation, whatever it may be, and is overloved if a shadow of excuse can be found.

"And indeed it's an absurd thing," I began, clearness of my argument, "why, he could not have warming to my task and admiring the extraordinary come; you have muddled and confused me, Nastenka, so that I too, have lost count of the time.... Only think: he can scarcely have received the letter; suppose he is not able to come, suppose he is going to answer the letter, could not come before to-morrow. I will go for it as soon as it's light to-morrow and let you know at once. Consider, there are thousands of possibilities; perhaps he was not at home when the letter came, and may not have read it even now! Anything may happen, you know."

"Yes, yes!" said Nastenka. "I did not think of that. Of course anything may happen?" she went on in a tone that offered no opposition, though some other far-away thought could be heard like a vexatious discord in it. "I tell you what you must do," she said, "you go as early as possible to-morrow morning, and if you get anything let me know at once. You know where I live, don't you?"

And she began repeating her address to me.

Then she suddenly became so tender, so solicitous with me. She seemed to listen attentively to what I told her; but when I asked her some question she was silent, was confused, and turned her head away. I looked into her eyes-yes, she was crying.

"How can you? How can you? Oh, what a baby you are! what childishness!... Come, come!"

She tried to smile, to calm herself, but her chin was quivering and her bosom was still heaving.

"I was thinking about you," she said after a minute's silence. "You are so kind that I should be a stone if I did not feel it. Do you know what has occurred to me now? I was comparing you two. Why isn't he you? Why isn't he like you? He is not as good as you, though I love him more than you."

I made no answer. She seemed to expect me to say something.

"Of course, it may be that I don't understand him fully yet. You know I was always as it were afraid of him; he was always so grave, as it were so proud. Of course I know it's only that he seems like that, I know there is more tenderness in his heart than in mine.... I remember how he looked at me when I went in to him—do you remember?—with my bundle; but yet I respect him too much, and doesn't that show that we are not equals?"

"No, Nastenka, no," I answered, "it shows that you love him more than anything in the world, and far more than yourself."

"Yes, supposing that is so," answered Nastenka naïvely. "But do you know what strikes me now? Only I am not talking about him now, but speaking generally; all this came into my mind some time ago. Tell me, how is it that we can't all be like brothers together? Why is it that even the best of men always seem to hide something from other people and to keep something back? Why not say straight out what is in one's heart, when one knows that one is not speaking idly? As it is every one seems harsher than he really is, as though all were afraid of doing injustice to their feelings, by being too quick to express them."

"Oh. Nastenka, what you say is true; but there are many reasons for that." I broke in suppressing my own feelings at that moment more than ever.

"No, no!" she answered with deep feeling. "Here you, for instance, are not like other people! I really don't know how to tell you what I feel; but it seems to me that you, for instance... at the present moment... it seems to me that you are sacrificing something for me," she added timidly, with a fleeting glance at me, "Forgive me for saying so, I am a simple girl you know, I have seen very little of life, and I really sometimes don't know how to say things," she added in a voice that quivered with some hidden feeling, while she tried to smile; "but I only wanted to tell you that I am grateful, that I feel it all too.... Oh, may God give you happiness for it! What you told me about your dreamer is quite untrue now—that is, I mean, it's not true of you. You are recovering, you are quite a different man from what you described. If you ever fall in love with some one, God give you happiness with her! I won't wish anything for her, for she will be happy with you. I know, I am a woman myself, so you must believe me when I tell you so."

She ceased speaking, and pressed my hand warmly. I too could not speak without emotion. Some minutes passed.

"Yes, it's clear he won't come to-night," she said at last raising her head. "It's late."

"He will come to-morrow," I said in the most firm and convincing tone.

"Yes," she added with no sign of her former depression. "I see for myself now that he could not come till to-morrow. Well, good-bye, till to-morrow. If it rains perhaps I shall not come. But the day after to-morrow, I shall come. I shall come for certain, whatever happens; be sure to be here, I want to see you, I will tell you everything."

And then when we parted she gave me her hand and said, looking at me candidly: "We shall always be together, shan't we?"

Oh, Nastenka, Nastenka! If only you knew how lonely I am now!

As soon as it struck nine o'clock I could not stay indoors, but put on my things, and went out in spite of the weather. I was there, sitting on our seat. I went to her street, but I felt ashamed, and turned back without looking at their windows, when I was two steps from her door. I went home more depressed than I had ever been before. What a damp, dreary day! If it had been fine I should have walked about all night....

But to-morrow, to-morrow! To-morrow she will tell me everything. The letter has not come to-day, however. But that was to be expected. They are together by now....

Fourth Night

My God, how it has all ended! What it has all ended in! I arrived at nine o'clock. She was already there. I noticed her a good way off; she was standing as she had been that first time, with her elbows on the railing, and she did not hear me coming up to her.

"Nastenka!" I called to her, suppressing my agitation with an effort.

She turned to me quickly.

"Well?" she said. "Well? Make haste!"

I looked at her in perplexity.

"Well, where is the letter? Have you brought the letter?" she repeated clutching at the railing.

"No, there is no letter," I said at last. "Hasn't he been to you yet?" She turned fearfully pale and looked at me for a long time without moving. I had shattered her last hope.

"Well, God be with him," she said at last in a breaking voice; "God be with him if he leaves me like that."

She dropped her eyes, then tried to look at me and could not. For several minutes she was struggling with her emotion. All at once she turned away, leaning her elbows against the railing and burst into tears.

"Oh don't, don't!" I began; but looking at her I had not the heart to go on, and what was I to say to her?

"Don't try and comfort me," she said; "don't talk about him; don't tell me that he will come, that he has not cast me off so cruelly and so inhumanly as he has. What for–what for? Can there have been something in my letter, that unlucky letter?"

At that point sobs stifled her voice; my heart was torn as I looked at her.

"Oh, how inhumanly cruel it is!" she began again.

"And not a line, not a line! He might at least have written that he does not want me, that he rejects me–but not a line for three days! How easy it is for him to wound, to insult a poor, defenceless girl, whose only fault is that she loves him! Oh, what I've suffered during these three days! Oh, dear! When I think that I was the first to go to him, that I humbled myself before him, cried, that I begged of him a little love!... and after that! Listen," she said, turning to me, and her black eyes flashed, "it isn't sol It can't be so; it isn't natural. Either you are mistaken or I; perhaps he has not received the letter? Perhaps he still knows nothing about it? How could any one–judge for yourself, tell me, for goodness' sake explain it to me, I can't understand it–how could any one behave with such barbarous coarseness as he has behaved to me? Not one word! Why, the lowest creature on earth is treated more compassionately. Perhaps he has heard something, perhaps some one has told him something about me," she cried, turning to me inquiringly: "What do you think?"

"Listen, Nastenka, I shall go to him to-morrow in your name."

"Yes?"

"I will question him about everything; I will tell him everything."

"Yes, yes?

"You write a letter. Don't say no, Nastenka, don't say no! I will make him respect your action, he shall hear all about it, and if–"

“No, my friend, no," she interrupted. "Enough! Not another word, not another line from me enough! I don't know him; I don't love him any more. I will forget him."

She could not go on.

"Calm yourself, calm yourself! Sit here, Nastenka," I said, making her sit down on the seat.

"I am calm. Don't trouble. It's nothing! It's only tears, they will soon dry. Why, do you imagine I shall do away with myself, that I shall throw myself into the river?"

My heart was full: I tried to speak, but I could not.

"Listen," she said taking my hand. "Tell me: you wouldn't have behaved like this, would you? You would not have abandoned a girl who had come to you of herself, you would not have thrown into her face a shameless taunt at her weak foolish heart? You would have taken care of her? You would have realized that she was alone, that she did not know how to look after herself, that she could not guard herself from loving you, that it was not her fault, not her fault–that she had done nothing.... Oh dear, oh dear!"

"Nastenka!" I cried at last, unable to control my emotion. "Nastenka, you torture me! You wound my heart, you are killing me, Nastenka! I cannot be silent! I must speak at last, give utterance to what is surging in my heart!"

As I said this I got up from the seat. She took my hand and looked at me in surprise.

"What is the matter with you?" she said at last.

"Listen," I said resolutely. "Listen to me, Nastenka! What I am going to say to you now is all nonsense, all impossible, all stupid! I know that this can never be, but I cannot be silent. For the sake of what you are suffering now, I beg you beforehand to forgive me!"

"What is it? What is it?" she said drying her tears and looking at me intently, while a strange curiosity gleamed in her astonished eyes. "What is the matter?"

"It's impossible, but I love you, Nastenka! There it is! Now everything is told," I said with a wave of my hand. "Now you will see whether you can go on talking to me as you did just now, whether you can listen to what I am going to say to you."...

"Well, what then?" Nastenka interrupted me. "What of it? I knew you loved me long ago, only I always thought that you simply liked me very much.... Oh dear, oh dear!"

"At first it was simply liking, Nastenka, but now, now! I am just in the same position as you were when you went to him with your bundle. In a worse position than you, Nastenka, because he cared for no one else as you do."

"What are you saying to me! I don't understand you in the least. But tell me, what's this for; I don't mean what for, but why are you... so suddenly.... Oh dear, I am talking nonsense! But you...."

And Nastenka broke off in confusion. Her cheeks flamed; she dropped her eyes.

"What's to be done, Nastenka, what am I to do? I am to blame. I have abused your.... But no, no, I am not to blame, Nastenka; I feel that, I know that, because my heart tells me I am right, for I cannot hurt you in any way, I cannot wound you! I was your friend, but I am still your friend, I have betrayed no trust. Here my tears are falling, Nastenka. Let them flow, let them flow–they don't hurt anybody. They will dry, Nastenka."

"Sit down, sit down," she said, making me sit down on the seat. "Oh, my God!"

"No, Nastenka, I won't sit down; I cannot stay here any longer, you cannot see me again; I will tell you everything and go away. I only want to say that you would never have found out that I loved you. I should have kept my secret. I would not have worried you at such a moment with my egoism. No! But I could not resist it now; you spoke of it yourself, it is your fault, your fault and not mine. You cannot drive me away from you."...

"No, no, I don't drive you away, no!" said Nastenka, concealing her confusion as best she could, poor child.

"You don't drive me away? No! But I meant to run from you myself. I will go away, but first I will tell you all, for when you were crying here I could not sit unmoved, when you wept, when you were in torture at being–at being–I will speak of it, Nastenka–at being forsaken, at your love being repulsed, I felt that in my heart there was so much love for you, Nastenka, so much love! And it seemed so bitter that I could not help you with my love, that my heart was breaking and I... I could not be silent, I had to speak, Nastenka, I had to speak!"

"Yes, yes! tell me, talk to me," said Nastenka with an indescribable gesture. "Perhaps you think it strange that I talk to you like this, but... speak! I will tell you afterwards! I will tell you everything."

"You are sorry for me, Nastenka, you are simply sorry for me, my dear little friend! What's done can't be mended. What is said cannot be taken back. Isn't that so? Well, now you know. That's the starting-point. Very well. Now it's all right, only listen. When you were sitting crying I thought to myself (oh, let me tell you what I was thinking!), I thought, that (of course it cannot be, Nastenka), I thought that you... I thought that you somehow... quite apart from me, had ceased to love him. Then–I thought that yesterday and the day before yesterday, Nastenka–then I would–I certainly would–have succeeded in making you love me; you know, you said yourself, Nastenka, that you almost loved me. Well, what next? Well, that's nearly all I wanted to tell you; all that is left to say is how it would be if you loved me, only that, nothing more! Listen, my friend–for any way you are my friend–I am, of course, a poor, humble man, of no great consequence; but that's not the point (I don't seem to be able to say what I mean, Nastenka, I am so confused), only I would love you, I would love you so, that even if you still loved him, even if you went on loving the man I don't know, you would never feel that my love was a burden to you. You would only feel every minute that at your side was beating a grateful, grateful heart, a warm heart ready for your sake.... Oh Nastenka, Nastenka! What have you done to me?"

"Don't cry; I don't want you to cry," said Nastenka getting up quickly from the seat. "Come along, get up, come with me, don't cry, don't cry," she said, drying her tears with her handkerchief; "let us go now, maybe I will tell you something.... If he has forsaken me now, if he has forgotten me, though I still love him (I do not want to deceive you)...

but listen, answer me. If I were to love you, for instance, that is, if I only.... Oh my friend, my friend! To think, to think how I wounded you, when I laughed at your love, when I praised you for not falling in love with me. Oh dear! How was it I did not foresee this, how was it I did not foresee this, how could I have been so stupid? But.... Well, I have made up my mind, I will tell you."

"Look here, Nastenka, do you know what? I'll go away, that's what I'll do. I am simply tormenting you. Here you are remorseful for having laughed at me, and I won't have you ... in addition to your sorrow.... Of course it is my fault, Nastenka, but good-bye!"

"Stay, listen to me: can you wait?"

"What for? How?"

"I love him; but I shall get over it, I must get over it, I cannot fail to get over it; I am getting over it, I feel that.... Who knows? Perhaps it will all end to-day, for I hate him, for he has been laughing at me, while you have been weeping here with me, for you have not repulsed me as he has, for you love me while he has never loved me, for in fact, I love you myself.... Yes, I love you! I love you as you love me; I have told you so before, you heard it yourself–I love you because you are better than he is, because you are nobler than he is, because, because he——"

The poor girl's emotion was so violent that she could not say more; she laid her head upon my shoulder, then upon my bosom, and wept bitterly. I comforted her, I persuaded her, but she could not stop crying; she kept pressing my hand, and saying between her sobs: "Wait, wait, it will be over in a minute! I want to tell you... you mustn't think that these tears–it's nothing, it's weakness, wait till it's over."... At last she left off crying, dried her eyes and we walked on again. I wanted to speak, but she still begged me to wait. We were silent.... At last she plucked up courage and began to speak.

"It's like this," she began in a weak and quivering voice, in which, however, there was a note that pierced my heart with a sweet pang; "don't think that I am so light and inconstant, don't think that I can forget and change so quickly. I have loved him for a whole year, and I swear by God that I have never, never, even in thought, been unfaithful to him.... He has despised me, he has been laughing at me–God forgive him! But he has insulted me and wounded my heart. I... I do not love him, for I can only love what is magnanimous, what understands me, what is generous; for I am like that myself and he is not worthy of me–well, that's enough of him. He has done better than if he had deceived my expectations later, and shown me later what he was.... Well, it's over! But who knows, my dear friend," she went on pressing my hand, "who knows, perhaps my whole love was a mistaken feeling, a delusion–perhaps it began in mischief, in nonsense, because I was kept so strictly by grandmother? Perhaps I ought to love another man, not him, a different man, who would have pity on me and ... and.... But don't let us say any more about that," Nastenka broke off, breathless with emotion. I only wanted to tell you ... I wanted to tell you that if, although I love him (no, did love him), if, in spite of this you still say.... If you feel that your love is so great that it may at last drive from my heart my old feeling if–you will have pity on me–if you do not want to leave me alone to my fate, without hope, without consolation–if you are ready to love me always as you do now–I swear to you that gratitude... that my love will be at last worthy of your love.... Will you take my hand?"

"Nastenka!" I cried breathless with sobs. "Nastenka, oh Nastenka!"

"Enough, enough! Well, now it's quite enough," she said, hardly able to control herself. "Well, now all has been said, hasn't it! Hasn't it? You are happy–I am happy too. Not another word about it, wait; spare me... talk of something else, for God's sake."

"Yes, Nastenka, yes! Enough about that, now I am happy. I—— Yes, Nastenka, yes, let us talk of other things, let us make haste and talk. Yes! I am ready."

And we did not know what to say: we laughed, we wept, we said thousands of things meaningless and incoherent; at one moment we walked along the pavement, then suddenly turned back and crossed the road; then we stopped and went back again to the embankment; we were like children.

"I am living alone now, Nastenka," I began, "but to-morrow! Of course you know, Nastenka, I am poor, I have only got twelve hundred roubles, but that doesn't matter."

"Of course not, and granny has her pension, so she will be no burden. We must take granny."

"Of course we must take granny. But there's Matrona."

"Yes, and we've got Fyokla too!"

"Matrona is a good woman, but she has one fault: she has no imagination, Nastenka, absolutely none; but that doesn't matter."

"That's all right-they can live together; only you must move to us to-morrow."

"To you? How so? All right, I am ready."

"Yes, hire a room from us. We have a top floor, it's empty. We had an old lady lodging there, but she has gone away; and I know granny would like to have a young man. I said to her, 'Why a young man?' And she said, 'Oh, because I am old; only don't you fancy, Nastenka, that I want him as a husband for you.' So I guessed it was with that idea."

"Oh, Nastenka!"

And we both laughed.

"Come, that's enough, that's enough. But where do you live? I've forgotten."

"Over that way, near X bridge, Barannikov's Buildings."

"It's that big house?"

"Yes, that big house."

"Oh, I know, a nice house; only you know you had better give it up and come to us as soon as possible."

"To-morrow, Nastenka, to-morrow; I owe a little for my rent there but that doesn't matter. I shall soon get my salary."

"And do you know I will perhaps give lessons; I will learn something myself and then give lessons."

"Capital! And I shall soon get a bonus."

"So by to-morrow you will be my lodger.

"And we will go to The Barber of Seville, for they are soon going to give it again."

"Yes, we'll go," said Nastenka, "but better see something else and not The Barber of Seville."

"Very well, something else. Of course that will be better, I did not think——"

As we talked like this we walked along in a sort of delirium, a sort of intoxication, as though we did not know what was happening to us. At one moment we stopped and talked for a long time at the same place; then we went on again, and goodness knows where we went; and again tears and again laughter. All of a sudden Nastenka would want to go home, and I would not dare to detain her but would want to see her to the house; we set off, and in a quarter of an hour found ourselves at the embankment by our seat. Then she would sigh, and tears would come into her eyes again; I would turn chill with dismay.... But she would press my hand and force me to walk, to talk, to chatter as before.

"It's time I was home at last; I think it must be very late, Nastenka said at last. "We must give over being childish."

"Yes, Nastenka, only I shan't sleep to-night; I am not going home."

"I don't think I shall sleep either; only see me home."

"I should think so!"

"Only this time we really must get to the house."

"We must, we must."

"Honour bright? For you know one must go home some time!"

"Honour bright," I answered laughing.

"Well, come along!"

"Come along! Look at the sky, Nastenka. Look! To-morrow it will be a lovely day; what a blue sky, what a moon! Look; that yellow cloud is covering it now, look, look! No, it has passed by. Look, look!"

But Nastenka did not look at the cloud; she stood mute as though turned to stone; a minute later she huddled timidly close up to me. Her hand trembled in my hand; I looked at her. She pressed still more closely to me.

At that moment a young man passed by us. He suddenly stopped, looked at us intently, and then again took a few steps on. My heart began throbbing.

"Who is it, Nastenka?" I said in an undertone.

"It's he," she answered in a whisper, huddling up to me, still more closely, still more tremulously.... I could hardly stand on my feet.

"Nastenka, Nastenka! It's you!" I heard a voice behind us and at the same moment the young man took several steps towards us.

My God, how she cried out! How she started! How she tore herself out of my arms and rushed to meet him! I stood and looked at them, utterly crushed. But she had hardly given him her hand, had hardly flung herself into his arms, when she turned to me again, was beside me again in a flash, and before I knew where I was she threw both arms round my neck and gave me a warm, tender kiss. Then, without saying a word to me, she rushed back to him again, took his hand, and drew him after her.

I stood a long time looking after them. At last the two vanished from my sight.

Morning

My night ended with the morning. It was a wet day. The rain was falling and beating disconsolately upon my window pane; it was dark in the room and grey outside. My head ached and I was giddy; fever was stealing over my limbs.

"There's a letter for you, sir; the postman brought it," Matrona said stooping over me.

"A letter? From whom?" I cried jumping up from my chair.

"I don't know, sir, better look–maybe it is written there whom it is from."

I broke the seal. It was from her!

*****

"Oh, forgive me, forgive me! I beg you on my knees to forgive me! I deceived you and myself. It was a dream, a mirage.... My heart aches for you to-day; forgive me, forgive me!

"Don't blame me, for I have not changed to you in the least. I told you that I would love you, I love you now, I more than love you. Oh, my God! If only I could love you both at once! Oh, if only you were he!"

["Oh, if only he were you," echoed in my mind. I remembered your words, Nastenka!]

"God knows what I would do for you now! I know that you are sad and dreary. I have wounded you, but you know when one loves a wrong is soon forgotten. And you love me.

"Thank you, yes, thank you for that love! For it will live in my memory like a sweet dream which lingers long after awakening; for I shall remember for ever that instant when you opened your heart to me like a brother and so generously accepted the gift of my shattered heart to care for it, nurse it, and heal it.... If you forgive me, the memory of you will be exalted by a feeling of everlasting gratitude which will never be effaced from my soul.... I will treasure that memory: I will be true to it, I will not betray it, I will not betray my heart: it is too constant. It returned so quickly yesterday to him to whom it has always belonged.

"We shall meet, you will come to us, you will not leave us, you will be for ever a friend, a brother to me. And when you see me you will give me your hand... yes? You will give it to me, you have forgiven me, haven't you? You love me as before?

"Oh, love me, do not forsake me, because I love you so at this moment, because I am worthy of your love, because I will deserve it... my dear! Next week I am to be married to him. He has come back in love, he has never forgotten me. You will not be angry at my writing about him. But I want to come and see you with him; you will like him, won't you?

"Forgive me, remember and love your.

Nastenka

I read that letter over and over again for a long time; tears gushed to my eyes. At last it fell from my hands and I hid my face.

"Dearie! I say, dearie——" Matrona began.

"What is it, Matrona?"

"I have taken all the cobwebs off the ceiling; you can have a wedding or give a party."

I looked at Matrona. She was still a hearty, youngish old woman, but I don't know why all at once I suddenly pictured her with lustreless eyes, a wrinkled face, bent, decrepit.... I don't know why I suddenly pictured my room grown old like Matrona. The walls and the floors looked discoloured, everything seemed dingy; the spiders' webs were thicker than ever. I don't know why, but when I looked out of the window it seemed to me that the house opposite had grown old and dingy too, that the stucco on the columns was peeling off and crumbling, that the cornices were cracked and blackened, and that the walls, of a vivid deep yellow, were patchy.

Either the sunbeams suddenly peeping out from the clouds for a moment were hidden again behind a veil of rain, and everything had grown dingy again before my eyes; or perhaps the whole vista of my future flashed before me so sad and forbidding, and I saw myself just as I was now, fifteen years hence, older, in the same room, just as solitary, with the same Matrona grown no cleverer for those fifteen years.

But to imagine that I should bear you a grudge, Nastenka! That I should cast a dark cloud over your serene, untroubled happiness; that by my bitter reproaches I should cause distress to your heart, should poison it with secret remorse and should force it to throb with anguish at the moment of bliss; that I should crush a single one of those tender blossoms which you have twined in your dark tresses when you go with him to the altar.... Oh never, never! May your sky be clear, may your sweet smile be bright and untroubled, and may you be blessed for that moment of blissful happiness which you gave to another, lonely and grateful heart!

My God, a whole moment of happiness! Is that too little for the whole of a man's life?

A Faint Heart
(A Story)

Under the same roof in the same flat on the same fourth storey lived two young men, colleagues in the service, Arkady Ivanovitch Nefedevitch and Vasya Shumkov.... The author of course, feels the necessity of explaining to the reader why one is given his full title, while the other's name is abbreviated, if only that such a mode of expression may not be regarded as unseemly and rather familiar. But, to do so, it would first be necessary to explain and describe the rank and years and calling and duty in the service, and even, indeed, the characters of the persons concerned; and since there are so many writers who begin in that way, the author of the proposed story, solely in order to be unlike them (that is, some people will perhaps say, entirely on account of his boundless vanity), decides to begin straightaway with action. Having completed this introduction, he begins.

Towards six o'clock on New Year's Eve Shumkov returned home. Arkady Ivanovitch, who was lying on the bed, woke up and looked at his friend with half-closed eyes. He saw that Vasya had on his very best trousers and a very clean shirt front. That, of course, struck him. "Where had Vasya to go like that? And he had not dined at home either!" Meanwhile, Shumkov had lighted a candle, and Arkady Ivanovitch guessed immediately that his friend was intending to wake him accidentally. Vasya did, in fact, clear his throat twice, walked twice up and down the room, and at last, quite accidentally, let the pipe, which he had begun filling in the corner by the stove, slip out of his hands. Arkady Ivanovitch laughed to himself.

"Vasya, give over pretending!" he said.

"Arkasha, you are not asleep?"

"I really cannot say for certain; it seems to me I am not."

"Oh, Arkasha! How are you, dear boy? Well, brother! Well, brother!... You don't know what I have to tell you!"

"I certainly don't know; come here."

As though expecting this, Vasya went up to him at once, not at all anticipating, however, treachery from Arkady Ivanovitch. The other seized him very adroitly by the arms, turned him over, held him down, and began, as it is called, "strangling" his victim, and apparently this proceeding afforded the lighthearted Arkady Ivanovitch great satisfaction.

"Caught!" he cried. "Caught!"

"Arkasha, Arkasha, what are you about? Let me go. For goodness sake, let me go, I shall crumple my dress coat!"

"As though that mattered! What do you want with a dress coat? Why were you so confiding as to put yourself in my hands? Tell me, where have you been? Where have you dined?"

"Arkasha, for goodness sake, let me go!"

"Where have you dined?"

"Why, it's about that I want to tell you."

"Tell away, then.

"But first let me go.

"Not a bit of it, I won't let you go till you tell me!

"Arkasha! Arkasha! But do you understand, I can't–it is utterly impossible! cried Vasya, helplessly wriggling out of his friend's powerful clutches, you know there are subjects!

"How–subjects?"...

"Why, subjects that you can't talk about in such a position without losing your dignity; it's utterly impossible; it would make it ridiculous, and this is not a ridiculous matter, it is important."

"Here, he's going in for being important! That's a new idea! You tell me so as to make me laugh, that's how you must tell me; I don't want anything important; or else you are no true friend of mine. Do you call yourself a friend? Eh?"

"Arkasha, I really can't!"

"Well, I don't want to hear...."

"Well, Arkasha!" began Vasya, lying across the bed and doing his utmost to put all the dignity possible into his words. "Arkasha! If you like, I will tell you; only...."

"Well, what?..."

"Well, I am engaged to be married!"

Without uttering another word Arkady Ivanovitch took Vasya up in his arms like a baby, though the latter was by no means short, but rather long and thin, and began dexterously carrying him up and down the room, pretending that he was hushing him to sleep.

"I'll put you in your swaddling clothes, Master Bridegroom," he kept saying. But seeing that Vasya lay in his arms, not stirring or uttering a word, he thought better of it at once, and reflecting that the joke had gone too far, set him down in the middle of the room and kissed him on the cheek in the most genuine and friendly way.

"Vasya, you are not angry?"

"Arkasha, listen...."

"Come, it's New Year's Eve."

"Oh, I'm all right; but why are you such a madman, such a scatterbrain? How many times I have told you: Arkasha, it's really not funny, not funny at all!"

"Oh, well, you are not angry?"

"Oh, I'm all right; am I ever angry with any one! But you have wounded me, do you understand?"

"But how have I wounded you? In what way?"

"I come to you as to a friend, with a full heart, to pour out my soul to you, to tell you of my happiness...."

"What happiness? Why don't you speak?..."

"Oh, well, I am going to get married!" Vasya answered with vexation, for he really was a little exasperated.

"You! You are going to get married! So you really mean it?" Arkasha cried at the top of his voice. "No, no ... but what's this? He talks like this and his tears are flowing.... Vasya, my little Vasya, don't, my little son! Is it true, really?" And Arkady Ivanovitch flew to hug him again.

"Well, do you see, how it is now?" said Vasya. "You are kind, of course, you are a friend, I know that. I come to you with such joy, such rapture, and all of a sudden I have to disclose all the joy of my heart, all my rapture struggling across the bed, in an undignified way.... You understand, Arkasha, Vasya went on, half laughing. "You see, it made it seem comic: and in a sense I did not belong to myself at that minute. I could not let this be slighted.... What's more, if you had asked me her name, I swear, I would sooner you killed me than have answered you."

"But, Vasya, why did you not speak! You should have told me all about it sooner and I would not have played the fool!" cried Arkady Ivanovitch in genuine despair.

"Come, that's enough, that's enough! Of course, that's how it is.... You know what it all comes from–from my having a good heart. What vexes me is, that I could not tell you as I wanted to, making you glad and happy, telling you nicely and initiating you into my secret properly.... Really, Arkasha, I love you so much that I believe if it were not for you I shouldn't be getting married, and, in fact, I shouldn't be living in this world at all!"

Arkady Ivanovitch, who was excessively sentimental, cried and laughed at once as he listened to Vasya. Vasya did the same. Both flew to embrace one another again and forgot the past.

"How is it–how is it? Tell me all about it, Vasya! I am astonished, excuse me, brother, but I am utterly astonished; it's a perfect thunderbolt, by Jove! Nonsense, nonsense, brother, you have made it up, you've really made it up, you are telling fibs!" cried Arkady Ivanovitch, and he actually looked into Vasya's face with genuine uncertainty, but seeing in it the radiant confirmation of a positive intention of being married as soon as possible, threw himself on the bed and began rolling from side to side in ecstasy till the walls shook.

"Vasya, sit here," he said at last, sitting down on the bed.

"I really don't know, brother, where to begin!"

They looked at one another in joyful excitement.

"Who is she, Vasya?"

"The Artemyevs!..." Vasya pronounced, in a voice weak with emotion.

"No?"

"Well, I did buzz into your ears about them at first, and then I shut up, and you noticed nothing. Ah, Arkasha, if you knew how hard it was to keep it from you; but I was afraid, afraid to speak! I thought it would all go wrong, and you know I was in love, Arkasha! My God! my God! You see this was the trouble," he began, pausing continually from agitation, "she had a suitor a year ago, but he was suddenly ordered somewhere; I knew him–he was a fellow, bless him! Well, he did not write at all, he simply vanished. They waited and waited, wondering what it meant.... Four months ago he suddenly came back married, and has never set foot within their doors! It was coarse–shabby! And they had no one to stand up for them. She cried and cried, poor girl, and I fell in love with her... indeed, I had been in love with her long before, all the time! I began comforting her, and was always going there.... Well, and I really don't know how it has all come about, only she came to love me; a week ago I could not restrain myself, I cried, I sobbed, and told her everything–well, that I love her–everything, in fact!... 'I am ready to love you, too, Vassily Petrovitch, only I am a poor girl, don't make a mock of me; I don't dare to love any one.' Well, brother, you understand! You understand?... On that we got engaged on the spot. I kept thinking and thinking and thinking and thinking, I said to her, 'How are we to tell your mother?' She said, 'It will be hard, wait a little; she's afraid, and now maybe she would not let you have me; she keeps crying, too.' Without telling her I blurted it out to her mother to-day. Lizanka fell on her knees before her, I did the same well, she gave us her blessing. Arkasha, Arkashal My dear fellow! We will live together. No, I won't part from you for anything."

"Vasya, look at you as I may, I can't believe it. I don't believe it, I swear. I keep feeling as though.... Listen, how can you be engaged to be married?... How is it I didn't know, eh? Do you know, Vasya, I will confess it to you now. I was thinking of getting married myself; but now since you are going to be married, it is just as good! Be happy, be happy!..."

"Brother, I feel so lighthearted now, there is such sweetness in my soul..." said Vasya, getting up and pacing about the room excitedly. "Don't you feel the same? We shall be poor, of course, but we shall be happy; and you know it is not a wild fancy; our happiness is not a fairy tale; we shall be happy in reality!..."

"Vasya, Vasya, listen!"

"What?" said Vasya, standing before Arkady Ivanovitch.

"The idea occurs to me; I am really afraid to say it to you.... Forgive me, and settle my doubts. What are you going to live on? You know I am delighted that you are going to be married, of course, I am delighted, and I don't know what to do with myself, but-what are you going to live on? Eh?"

"Oh, good Heavens! What a fellow you are, Arkasha!" said Vasya, looking at Nefedevitch in profound astonishment. "What do you mean? Even her old mother, even she did not think of that for two minutes when I put it all clearly before her. You had better ask what they are living on! They have five hundred roubles a year between the three of them: the pension, which is all they have, since the father died. She and her old mother and her little brother, whose schooling is paid for out of that income too–that is how they live! It's you and I are the capitalists! Some good years it works out to as much as seven hundred for me."

"I say, Vasya, excuse me; I really... you know I ... I am only thinking how to prevent things going wrong. How do you mean, seven hundred? It's only three hundred...."

"Three hundred!... And Yulian Mastakovitch? Have you forgotten him?"

"Yulian Mastakovitch? But you know that's uncertain, brother; that's not the same thing as three hundred roubles of secure salary, where every rouble is a friend you can trust. Yulian Mastakovitch, of course, he's a great man, in fact, I respect him, I understand him, though he is so far above us; and, by Jove, I love him, because he likes you and gives you something for your work, though he might not pay you, but simply order a clerk to work for him–but you will agree, Vasya.... Let me tell you, too, I am not talking nonsense. I admit in all Petersburg you won't find a handwriting like your handwriting. I am ready to allow that to you," Nefedevitch concluded. not without enthusiasm. "But, God forbid! you may displease him all at once, you may not satisfy him. your work with him may stop, he may take another clerk–all sorts of things may happen, in fact! You know, Yulian Mastakovitch may be here to-day and gone to-morrow...."

"Well, Arkasha, the ceiling might fall on our heads this minute."

"Oh, of course, of course, I mean nothing."

"But listen, hear what I have got to say–you know, I don't see how he can part with me.... No, hear what I have to say! hear what I have to say! You see, I perform all my duties punctually; you know how kind he is, you know, Arkasha, he gave me fifty roubles in silver to-day!"

"Did he really, Vasya? A bonus for you?"

"Bonus, indeed, it was out of his own pocket. He said: 'Why, you have had no money for five months, brother, take some if you want it; thank you, I am satisfied with you.'... Yes, really! 'Yes, you don't work for me for nothing, said he. He did, indeed, that's what he said. It brought tears into my eyes, Arkasha. Good Heavens, yes!"

"I say, Vasya, have you finished copying those papers?..."

"No.... I haven't finished them yet."

"Vas...ya! My angell What have you been doing?"

"Listen, Arkasha, it doesn't matter, they are not wanted for another two days, I have time enough...."

"How is it you have not done them?"

"That's all right, that's all right. You look so horror-stricken that you turn me inside out and make my heart ache! You are always going on at me like this! He's for ever crying out: Oh, oh, oh!!! Only consider, what does it matter? Why, I shall finish it, of course I shall finish it...."

"What if you don't finish it?" cried Arkady, jumping up, "and he has made you a present to-day! And you going to be married.... Tut, tut, tut!..."

"It's all right, it's all right," cried Shumkov, "I shall sit down directly, I shall sit down this minute."

"How did you come to leave it, Vasya?"

"Oh, Arkasha! How could I sit down to work! Have I been in a fit state? Why, even at the office I could scarcely sit still, I could scarcely bear the beating of my heart.... Oh! oh! Now I shall work all night, and I shall work all to-morrow night, and the night after, too–and I shall finish it."

"Is there a great deal left?"

"Don't hinder me, for goodness' sake, don't hinder me; hold your tongue."

Arkady Ivanovitch went on tip-toe to the bed and sat down, then suddenly wanted to get up, but was obliged to sit down again, remembering that he might interrupt him, though he could not sit still for excitement: it was evident that the news had thoroughly upset him, and the first thrill of delight had not yet passed off. He glanced at Shumkov; the latter glanced at him, smiled, and shook his finger at him, then, frowning severely (as though all his energy and the success of his work depended upon it), fixed his eyes on the papers.

It seemed that he, too, could not yet master his emotion; he kept changing his pen, fidgeting in his chair, re-arranging things, and setting to work again, but his hand trembled and refused to move.

"Arkasha, I've talked to them about you," he cried suddenly, as though he had just remembered it.

"Yes," cried Arkasha, "I was just wanting to ask you that. Well?"

"Well, I'll tell you everything afterwards. Of course, it is my own fault, but it quite went out of my head that I didn't mean to say anything till I had written four pages, but I thought of you and of them. I really can't write, brother, I keep thinking about you...."

Vasya smiled.

A silence followed.

"Phew! What a horrid pen," cried Shumkov, flinging it on the table in vexation. He took another.

"Vasya! listen! one word...."

"Well, make haste, and for the last time."

"Have you a great deal left to do?"

"Ah, brother!" Vasya frowned, as though there could be nothing more terrible and murderous in the whole world than such a question. "A lot, a fearful lot."

"Do you know, I have an idea——"

"What?"

"Oh, never mind, never mind; go on writing."

"Why, what? what?"

"It's past six, Vasya."

Here Nefedevitch smiled and winked slyly at Vasya, though with a certain timidity, not knowing how Vasya would take it.

"Well, what is it?" said Vasya, throwing down his pen, looking him straight in the face and actually turning pale with excitement.

"Do you know what?"

"For goodness sake, what is it?"

"I tell you what, you are excited, you won't get much done.... Stop, stop, stop! I have it, I have it–listen," said Nefedevitch, jumping up from the bed in delight, preventing Vasya from speaking and doing his utmost to ward off all objections; "first of all you must get calm, you must pull yourself together, mustn't you?"

"Arkasha, Arkasha!" cried Vasya, jumping up from his chair, "I will work all night, I will, really."

"Of course, of course, you won't go to bed till morning."

"I won't go to bed, I won't go to bed at all."

"No, that won't do, that won't do: you must sleep, go to bed at five. I will call you at eight. To-morrow is a holiday; you can sit and scribble away all day long.... Then the night and–but have you a great deal left to do?"

"Yes, look, look!"

Vasya, quivering with excitement and suspense, showed the manuscript: "Look!"

"I say, brother, that's not much."

"My dear fellow, there's some more of it," said Vasya, looking very timidly at Nefedevitch, as though the decision whether he was to go or not depended upon the latter.

"How much?"

"Two signatures."

"Well, what's that? Come, I tell you what. We shall have time to finish it, by Jove, we shall!"

"Arkasha!"

"Vasya, listen! To-night, on New Year's Eve, every one is at home with his family. You and I are the only ones without a home or relations.... Oh, Vasya!"

Nefedevitch clutched Vasya and hugged him in his leonine arms.

"Arkasha, it's settled."

"Vasya, boy, I only wanted to say this. You see, Vasya–listen, bandy-legs, listen!..."

Arkady stopped, with his mouth open, because he could not speak for delight. Vasya held him by the shoulders, gazed into his face and moved his lips, as though he wanted to speak for him.

"Well," he brought out at last.

"Introduce me to them to-day."

"Arkady, let us go to tea there. I tell you what, I tell you what. We won't even stay to see in the New Year, we'll come away earlier," cried Vasya, with genuine inspiration.

"That is, we'll go for two hours, neither more nor less...."

"And then separation till I have finished...."

"Vasya, boy!"

"Arkady!"

Three minutes later Arkady was dressed in his best. Vasya did nothing but brush himself, because he had been in such haste to work that he had not changed his trousers.

They hurried out into the street, each more pleased than the other. Their way lay from the Petersburg Side to Kolomna. Arkady Ivanovitch stepped out boldly and vigorously, so that from his walk alone one could see how glad he was at the good fortune of his friend, who was more and more radiant with happiness. Vasya trotted along with shorter steps, though his deportment was none the less dignified. Arkady Ivanovitch, in fact, had never seen him before to such advantage. At that moment he actually felt more respect for him, and Vasya's physical defect, of which the reader is not yet aware (Vasya was slightly deformed), which always called forth a feeling of loving sympathy in Arkady Ivanovitch's kind heart, contributed to the deep tenderness the latter felt for him at this moment, a tenderness of which Vasya was in every way worthy. Arkady Ivanovitch felt ready to weep with happiness, but he restrained himself.

"Where are you going, where are you going, Vasya? It is nearer this way," he cried, seeing that Vasya was making in the direction of Voznesenky.

"Hold your tongue, Arkasha."

"It really is nearer, Vasya."

"Do you know what, Arkasha?" Vasya began mysteriously, in a voice quivering with joy, "I tell you what, I want to take Lizanka a little present."

"What sort of present?"

"At the corner here, brother, is Madame Leroux's, a wonderful shop."

"Well."

"A cap, my dear, a cap; I saw such a charming little cap to-day. I inquired, I was told it was the façon Manon Lescaut–a delightful thing. Cherry-coloured ribbons, and if it is not dear... Arkasha, even if it is dear...."

"I think you are superior to any of the poets, Vasya. Come along."

They ran along, and two minutes later went into the shop. They were met by a black-eyed Frenchwoman with curls, who, from the first glance at her customers, became as joyous and happy as they, even happier, if one may say so. Vasya was ready to kiss Madame Leroux in his delight....

"Arkasha," he said in an undertone, casting a casual glance at all the grand and beautiful things on little wooden stands on the huge table, "lovely things! What's that? What's this? This one, for instance, this little sweet, do you see?" Vasya whispered, pointing to a charming cap further away, which was not the one he meant to buy, because he had already from afar descried and fixed his eyes upon the real, famous one, standing at the other end. He looked at it in such a way that one might have supposed some one was going to steal it, or as though the cap itself might take wings and fly into the air just to prevent Vasya from obtaining it.

"Look," said Arkady Ivanovitch, pointing to one, "I think that's better."

"Well, Arkasha, that does you credit; I begin to respect you for your taste," said Vasya, resorting to cunning with Arkasha in the tenderness of his heart, "your cap is charming, but come this way."

"Where is there a better one, brother?"

"Look; this way."

"That," said Arkady, doubtfully.

But when Vasya, incapable of restraining himself any longer, took it from the stand from which it seemed to fly spontaneously, as though delighted at falling at last into the hands of so good a customer, and they heard the rustle of its ribbons, ruches and lace, an unexpected cry of delight broke from the powerful chest of Arkady Ivanovitch. Even Madame Leroux, while maintaining her incontestable dignity and pre-eminence in matters of taste, and remaining mute from condescension, rewarded Vasya with a smile of complete approbation, everything in her glance, gesture and smile saying at once: "Yes, you have chosen rightly, and are worthy of the happiness which awaits you."

"It has been dangling its charms in coy seclusion," cried Vasya, transferring his tender feelings to the charming cap. "You have been hiding on purpose, you sly little pet!" And he kissed it, that is the air surrounding it, for he was afraid to touch his treasure.

"Retiring as true worth and virtue," Arkady added enthusiastically, quoting humorously from a comic paper he had read that morning. "Well, Vasya?"

"Hurrah, Arkasha! You are witty to-day. I predict you will make a sensation, as women say. Madame Leroux, Madame Leroux!"

"What is your pleasure?"

"Dear Madame Leroux."

Madame Leroux looked at Arkady Ivanovitch and smiled condescendingly.

"You wouldn't believe how I adore you at this moment.... Allow me to give you a kiss...." And Vasya kissed the shopkeeper.

She certainly at that moment needed all her dignity to maintain her position with such a madcap. But I contend that the innate, spontaneous courtesy and grace with which Madame Leroux received Vasya's enthusiasm, was equally befitting. She forgave him, and how tactfully, how graciously, she knew how to behave in the circumstances. How could she have been angry with Vasya?

"Madame Leroux, how much?"

"Five roubles in silver," she answered, straightening herself with a new smile.

"And this one, Madame Leroux?" said Arkady Ivanovitch, pointing to his choice.

"That one is eight roubles."

"There, you see–there, you see! Come, Madame Leroux, tell me which is nicer, more graceful, more charming, which of them suits you best?"

"The second is richer, but your choice c'est plus coquet."

"Then we will take it."

Madame Leroux took a sheet of very delicate paper, pinned it up, and the paper with the cap wrapped in it seemed even lighter than the paper alone. Vasya took it carefully, almost holding his breath, bowed to Madame Leroux, said something else very polite to her and left the shop.

"I am a lady's man, I was born to be a lady's man, said Vasya, laughing a little noiseless, nervous laugh and dodging the passers-by, whom he suspected of designs for crushing his precious cap.

"Listen, Arkady, brother," he began a minute later, and there was a note of triumph, of infinite affection in his voice. "Arkady, I am so happy, I am so happy!"

"Vasya! how glad I am, dear boy!"

"No, Arkasha, no. I know that there is no limit to your affection for me; but you cannot be feeling one-hundredth part of what I am feeling at this moment. My heart is so full, so full! Arkasha, I am not worthy of such happiness. I feel that, I am conscious of it. Why has it come to me?" he said, his voice full of stifled sobs. "What have I done to deserve it? Tell me. Look what lots of people, what lots of tears, what sorrow, what work-a-day life without a holiday, while I, I am loved by a girl like that, I.... But you will see her yourself immediately, you will appreciate her noble heart. I was born in a humble station, now I have a grade in the service and an independent income–my salary. I was born with a physical defect, I am a little deformed. See, she loves me as I am. Yulian Mastakovitch was so kind, so attentive, so gracious to-day; he does not often talk to me; he came up to me: 'Well, how goes it, Vasya' (yes, really, he called me Vasya), 'are you going to have a good time for the holiday, eh?' he laughed.

"'Well, the fact is, Your Excellency,' I have work to do, but then I plucked up courage and said: 'and maybe I shall have a good time, too, Your Excellency. I really said it. He gave me the money, on the spot, then he said a couple of words more to me. Tears came into my eyes, brother, I actually cried, and he, too, seemed touched, he patted me on the shoulder, and said: 'Feel always, Vasya, as you feel this now. '"

Vasya paused for an instant. Arkady Ivanovitch turned away, and he, too, wiped away a tear with his fist.

"And, and ..." Vasya went on, "I have never spoken to you of this, Arkady.... Arkady, you make me so happy with your affection, without you I could not live, no, no, don't say anything, Arkady, let me squeeze your hand, let me... tha...ank... you...." Again Vasya could not finish.

Arkady Ivanovitch longed to throw himself on Vasya's neck, but as they were crossing the road and heard almost in their ears a shrill: "Hi! there!" they ran frightened and excited to the pavement.

Arkady Ivanovitch was positively relieved. He set down Vasya's outburst of gratitude to the exceptional circumstances of the moment. He was vexed. He felt that he had done so little for Vasya hitherto. He felt actually ashamed of himself when Vasya began thanking him for so little. But they had all their lives before them, and Arkady Ivanovitch breathed more freely.

The Artemyevs had quite given up expecting them. The proof of it was that they had already sat down to tea! And the old, it seems, are sometimes more clear-sighted than the young, even when the young are so exceptional. Lizanka had very earnestly maintained, "He isn't coming, he isn't coming, Mamma; I feel in my heart he is not coming;" while her mother on the contrary declared "that she had a feeling that he would certainly come, that he would not stay away, that he would run round, that he could have no office work now, on New Year's Eve." Even as Lizanka opened the door she did not in the least expect to see them, and greeted them breathlessly, with her heart throbbing like a captured bird's, flushing and turning as red as a cherry, a fruit which she wonderfully resembled. Good Heavens, what a surprise it was! What a joyful "Oh!" broke from her lips. "Deceiver! My darling!" she cried, throwing her arms round Vasya's neck. But imagine her amazement, her sudden confusion: just behind Vasya, as though trying to hide behind his back, stood Arkady Ivanovitch, a trifle out of countenance. It must be admitted that he was awkward in the company of women, very awkward indeed, in fact on one occasion something occurred but of that later. You must put yourself in his place, however. There was nothing to laugh at; he was standing in the entry, in his goloshes and overcoat, and in a cap with flaps over the ears, which he would have hastened to pull off, but he had, all twisted round in a hideous way, a yellow knitted scarf, which, to make things worse, was knotted at the back. He had to disentangle all this, to take it off as quickly as possible, to show himself to more advantage, for there is no one who does not prefer to show himself to advantage. And then Vasya, vexatious insufferable Vasya, of course always the same dear kind Vasya, but now insufferable, ruthless Vasya. "Here," he shouted, "Lizanka, I have brought you my Arkady? What do you think of him? He is my best friend, embrace him, kiss him, Lizanka, give him a kiss in advance; afterwards you will know him better–you can take it back again."

Well, what, I ask you, was Arkady Ivanovitch to do? And he had only untwisted half of the scarf so far. I really am sometimes ashamed of Vasya's excess of enthusiasm; it is, of course, the sign of a good heart, but... it's awkward, not nice!

At last both went in.... The mother was unutterably delighted to make Arkady Ivanovitch's acquaintance, "she had heard so much about him, she had...." But she did not finish. A joyful "Oh!" ringing musically through the room interrupted her in the middle of a sentence. Good Heavens! Lizanka was standing before the cap which had suddenly been unfolded before her gaze; she clasped her hands with the utmost simplicity, smiling such a smile.... Oh, Heavens! why had not Madame Leroux an even lovelier cap?

Oh, Heavens! but where could you find a lovelier cap? It was quite first-rate. Where could you get a better one? I mean it seriously. This ingratitude on the part of lovers moves me, in fact, to indignation and even wounds me a little. Why, look at it for yourself, reader, look, what could be more beautiful than this little love of a cap? Come, look at it.... But, no, no, my strictures are uncalled for; they had by now all agreed with me; it had been a momentary aberration; the blindness, the delirium of feeling; I am ready to forgive them.... But then you must look.... You must excuse me, kind reader, I am still talking about the cap: made of tulle, light as a feather, a broad cherry-coloured ribbon covered with lace passing between the tulle and the ruche, and at the back two wide long ribbons–they would fall down a little below the nape of the neck.... All that the cap needed was to be tilted a little to the back of the head; come, look at it; I ask you, after that... but I see you are not looking... you think it does not matter. You are looking in a different direction.... You are looking at two big tears, big as pearls, that rose in two jet black eyes, quivered for one instant on the eyelashes, and then dropped on the ethereal tulle of which Madame Leroux's artistic masterpiece was composed.... And again I feel vexed, those two tears were scarcely a tribute to the cap.... No, to my mind, such a gift should be given in cool blood, as only then can its full worth be appreciated. I am, I confess, dear reader, entirely on the side of the cap.

They sat down–Vasya with Lizanka and the old mother with Arkady Ivanovitch; they began to talk, and Arkady Ivanovitch did himself credit, I am glad to say that for him. One would hardly, indeed, have expected it of him. After a couple of words about Vasya he most successfully turned the conversation to Yulian Mastakovitch, his patron. And he talked so cleverly, so cleverly that the subject was not exhausted for an hour. You ought to have seen with what dexterity, what tact, Arkady Ivanovitch touched upon certain peculiarities of Yulian Mastakovitch which directly or indirectly affected Vasya. The mother was fascinated, genuinely fascinated; she admitted it herself; she purposely called Vasya aside, and said to him that his friend was a most excellent and charming young man, and, what was of most account, such a serious, steady young man. Vasya almost laughed aloud with delight. He remembered how the serious Arkady had tumbled him on his bed for a quarter of an hour. Then the mother signed to Vasya to follow her quietly and cautiously into the next room. It must be admitted that she treated Lizanka rather unfairly: she behaved treacherously to her daughter, in the fullness of her heart, of course, and showed Vasya on the sly the present Lizanka was preparing to give him for the New Year. It was a paper-case, embroidered in beads and gold in a very choice design: on one side was depicted a stag, absolutely lifelike, running swiftly, and so well done! On the other side was the portrait of a celebrated General, also an excellent likeness. I cannot describe Vasya's raptures. Meanwhile, time was not being wasted in the parlour. Lizanka went straight up to Arkady Ivanovitch. She took his hand, she thanked him for something, and Arkady Ivanovitch gathered that she was referring to her precious Vasya. Lizanka was, indeed, deeply touched: she had heard that Arkady Ivanovitch was such a true friend of her betrothed, so loved him, so watched over him, guiding him at every step with helpful advice, that she, Lizanka, could hardly help thanking him, could not refrain from feeling grateful, and hoping that Arkady Ivanovitch might like her, if only half as well as Vasya. Then she began questioning him as to whether Vasya was careful of his health, expressed some apprehensions in regard to his marked impulsiveness of character, and his lack of knowledge of men and practical life; she said that she would in time watch over him religiously, that she would take care of and cherish his lot, and finally, she hoped that Arkady Ivanovitch would not leave them, but would live with them.

"We three shall live like one," she cried, with extremely naïve enthusiasm.

But it was time to go. They tried, of course, to keep them, but Vasya answered point blank that it was impossible. Arkady Ivanovitch said the same. The reason was, of course, inquired into, and it came out at once that there was work to be done entrusted to Vasya by Yulian Mastakovitch, urgent, necessary, dreadful work, which must be handed in on the morning of the next day but one, and that it was not only unfinished, but had been completely laid aside. The mamma sighed when she heard of this, while Lizanka was positively scared, and hurried Vasya off in alarm. The last kiss lost nothing from this haste; though brief and hurried it was only the more warm and ardent. At last they parted and the two friends set off home.

Both began at once confiding to each other their impressions as soon as they found themselves in the street. And could they help it? Indeed, Arkady Ivanovitch was in love, desperately in love, with Lizanka. And to whom could he better confide his feelings than to Vasya, the happy man himself. And so he did; he was not bashful, but confessed everything at once to Vasya. Vasya laughed heartily and was immensely delighted, and even observed that this was all that was needed to make them greater friends than ever. "You have guessed my feelings, Vasya, said Arkady Ivanovitch. "Yes, I love her as I love you; she will be my good angel as well as yours, for the radiance of your happiness will be shed on me, too, and I can bask in its warmth. She will keep house for me too, Vasya; my happiness will be in her hands. Let her keep house for me as she will for you. Yes, friendship for you is friendship for her; you are not separable for me now, only I shall have two beings like you instead of one...." Arkady paused in the fullness of his feelings, while Vasya was shaken to the depths of his being by his friend's words. The fact is, he had never expected anything of the sort from Arkady. Arkady Ivanovitch was not very great at talking as a rule, he was not fond of dreaming, either; now he gave way to the liveliest, freshest, rainbow-tinted day-dreams. "How I will protect and cherish you both," he began again. "To begin with, Vasya, I will be godfather to all your children, every one of them; and secondly, Vasya, we must bestir ourselves about the future. We must buy furniture, and take a lodging so that you and she and I can each have a little room to ourselves. Do you know, Vasya, I'll run about to-morrow and look at the notices, on the gates! Three .. no, two rooms, we should not need more. I really believe, Vasya, I talked nonsense this morning, there will be money enough; why, as soon as I glanced into her eyes I calculated at once that there would be enough to live on. It will all be for her. Oh, how we will work! Now, Vasya, we might venture up to twenty-five roubles for rent. A lodging is everything, brother. Nice rooms and at once a man is cheerful, and his dreams are of the brightest hues. And, besides, Lizanka will keep the purse for both of us: not a farthing will be wasted. Do you suppose I would go to a restaurant? What do you take me for? Not on any account. And then we shall get a bonus and reward, for we shall be zealous in the service–oh! how we shall work, like oxen toiling in the fields.... Only fancy," and Arkady Ivanovitch's voice was faint with pleasure, "all at once and quite unexpected, twenty-five or thirty roubles.... Whenever there's an extra, there'll be a cap or a scarf or a pair of little stockings. She must knit me a scarf; look what a horrid one I've got, the nasty yellow thing, it did me a bad turn to-day! And you wore a nice one, Vasya, to introduce me while I had my head in a halter.... Though never mind that now. And look here, I undertake all the silver. I am bound to give you some little present,–that will be an honour, that will flatter my vanity.... My bonuses won't fail me, surely; you don't suppose they would give them to Skorohodov? No fear, they won't be landed in that person's pocket. I'll buy you silver spoons, brother, good knives–not silver knives, but thoroughly good ones; and a waistcoat, that is a waistcoat for myself. I shall be best man, of course. Only now, brother, you must keep at it, you must keep at it. I shall stand over you with a stick, brother, to-day and to-morrow and all night; I shall worry you to work. Finish, make haste and finish, brother. And then again to spend the evening, and then again both of us happy; we will go in for loto. We will spend the evening there–oh, it's jolly! Oh, the devill How, vexing it is I can't help you. I should like to take it and write it all for you.... Why is it our handwriting is not alike?"

"Yes," answered Vasya. "Yes, I must make haste. I think it must be eleven o'clock; we must make haste.... To work!" And saying this, Vasya, who had been all the time alternately smiling and trying to interrupt with some enthusiastic rejoinder the flow of his friend's feelings, and had, in short, been showing the most cordial response, suddenly subsided, sank into silence, and almost ran along the street. It seemed as though some burdensome idea had suddenly chilled his feverish head; he seemed all at once dispirited.

Arkady Ivanovitch felt quite uneasy; he scarcely got an answer to his hurried questions from Vasya, who confined himself to a word or two, sometimes an irrelevant exclamation.

"Why, what is the matter with you, Vasya?" he cried at last, hardly able to keep up with him. "Can you really be so uneasy?"

"Oh, brother, that's enough chatter!" Vasya answered, with vexation.

"Don't be depressed, Vasya–come, come," Arkady interposed. "Why, I have known you write much more in a shorter time! What's the matter? You've simply a talent for it! You can write quickly in an emergency; they are not going to lithograph your copy. You've plenty of time!... The only thing is that you are excited now, and preoccupied, and the work won't go so easily."

Vasya made no reply, or muttered something to himself, and they both ran home in genuine anxiety.

Vasya sat down to the papers at once. Arkady Ivanovitch was quiet and silent; he noiselessly undressed and went to bed, keeping his eyes fixed on Vasya.... A sort of panic came over him.... "What is the matter with him?" he thought to himself, looking at Vasya's face that grew whiter and whiter, at his feverish eyes, at the anxiety that was betrayed in every movement he made, "why, his hand is shaking...what a stupid! Why did I not advise him to sleep for a couple of hours, till he had slept off his nervous excitement, any way." Vasya had just finished a page, he raised his eyes, glanced casually at Arkady and at once, looking down, took up his pen again.

"Listen, Vasya," Arkady Ivanovitch began suddenly, "wouldn't it be best to sleep a little now? Look, you are in a regular fever."

Vasya glanced at Arkady with vexation, almost with anger, and made no answer.

"Listen, Vasya, you'll make yourself ill."

Vasya at once changed his mind. "How would it be to have tea, Arkady?" he said.

"How so? Why?"

"It will do me good. I am not sleepy, I'm not going to bed! I am going on writing. But now I should like to rest and have a cup of tea, and the worst moment will be over."

"First-rate, brother Vasya, delightful! Just so. I was wanting to propose it myself. And I can't think why it did not occur to me to do so. But I say, Mavra won't get up, she won't wake for anything...."

"True."

"That's no matter, though," cried Arkady Ivanovitch, leaping out of bed. "I will set the samovar myself. It won't be the first time...."

Arkady Ivanovitch ran to the kitchen and set to work to get the samovar; Vasya meanwhile went on writing. Arkady Ivanovitch, moreover, dressed and ran out to the baker's, so that Vasya might have something to sustain him for the night. A quarter of an hour later the samovar was on the table. They began drinking tea, but conversation flagged. Vasya still seemed preoccupied.

"To-morrow," he said at last, as though he had just thought of it, "I shall have to take my congratulations for the New Year...."

"You need not go at all."

"Oh yes, brother, I must," said Vasya.

"Why, I will sign the visitors' book for you everywhere.... How can you? You work to-morrow. You must work to-night, till five o'clock in the morning, as I said, and then get to bed. Or else you will be good for nothing to-morrow. I'll wake you at eight o'clock, punctually."

"But will it be all right, your signing for me?" said Vasya, half assenting.

"Why, what could be better? Everyone does it."

"I am really afraid."

"Why, why?"

"It's all right, you know, with other people, but Yulian Mastakovitch ... he has been so kind to me, you know, Arkasha, and when he notices it's not my own signature——"

"Notices! why, what a fellow you are, really, Vasya! How could he notice?... Come, you know I can imitate your signature awfully well, and make just the same flourish to it, upon my word I can. What nonsense! Who would notice?"

Vasya, made no reply, but emptied his glass hurriedly.... Then he shook his head doubtfully.

"Vasya, dear boy! Ah, if only we succeed! Vasya, what's the matter with you, you quite frighten me! Do you know, Vasya, I am not going to bed now, I am not going to sleep! Show me, have you a great deal left?"

Vasya gave Arkady such a look that his heart sank, and his tongue failed him.

"Vasya, what is the matter? What are you thinking? Why do you look like that?"

"Arkady, I really must go to-morrow to wish Yulian Mastakovitch a happy New Year."

"Well, go then!" said Arkady, gazing at him open-eyed, in uneasy expectation. "I say, Vasya, do write faster; I am advising you for your good, I really am! How often Yulian Mastakovitch himself has said that what he likes particularly about your writing is its legibility. Why, it is all that Skoroplehin cares for, that writing should be good and distinct like a copy, so as afterwards to pocket the paper and take it home for his children to copy; he can't buy copybooks, the blockhead! Yulian Mastakovitch is always saying, always insisting: 'Legible, legible, legible!'... What is the matter? Vasya, I really don't know how to talk to you.....it quite frightens me... you crush me with your depression".

"It's all right, it's all right," said Vasya, and he fell back in his chair as though fainting. Arkady was alarmed.

"Will you have some water? Vasya! Vasya!"

"Don't, don't," said Vasya, pressing his hand. "I am all right, I only feel sad, I can't tell why. Better talk of something else; let me forget it."

"Calm yourself, for goodness' sake, calm yourself, Vasya. You will finish it all right, on my honour, you will. And even if you don't finish, what will it matter? You talk as though it were a crime!"

"Arkady," said Vasya, looking at his friend with such meaning that Arkady was quite frightened, for Vasya had never been so agitated before.... "If I were alone, as I used to be.... No! I don't mean that. I keep wanting to tell you as a friend, to confide in you.... But why worry you, though?... You see, Arkady, to some much is given, others do a little thing as I do. Well, if gratitude, appreciation, is expected of you... and you can't give it?"

"Vasya, I don't understand you in the least."

"I have never been ungrateful," Vasya went on softly, as though speaking to himself, "but if I am incapable of expressing all I feel, it seems as though ... it seems, Arkady, as though I am really ungrateful, and that's killing me."

"What next, what next! As though gratitude meant nothing more than your finishing that copy in time? Just think what you are saying, Vasya? Is that the whole expression of gratitude?"

Vasya sank into silence at once, and looked open-eyed at Arkady, as though his unexpected argument had settled all his doubts. He even smiled, but the same melancholy expression came back to his face at once. Arkady, taking this smile as a sign that all his uneasiness was over, and the look that succeeded it as an indication that he was determined to do better, was greatly relieved.

"Well, brother Arkasha, you will wake up," said Vasya, "keep an eye on me; if I fall asleep it will be dreadful. I'll set to work now.... Arkasha?"

"What?"

"Oh, it's nothing, I only ... I meant...."

Vasya settled himself, and said no more, Arkady got into bed. Neither of them said one word about their friends, the Artemyevs. Perhaps both of them felt that they had been a little to blame, and that they ought not to have gone for their jaunt when they did. Arkady soon fell asleep, still worried about Vasya. To his own surprise he woke up exactly at eight o'clock in the morning. Vasya was asleep in his chair with the pen in his hand, pale and exhausted; the candle had burnt out. Mavra was busy getting the samovar ready in the kitchen.

"Vasya, Vasya!" Arkady cried in alarm, "when did you fall asleep?"

Vasya opened his eyes and jumped up from his chair.

"Oh!" he cried, "I must have fallen asleep...."

He flew to the papers-everything was right; all were in order; there was not a blot of ink, nor spot of grease from the candle on them.

"I think I must have fallen asleep about six o'clock, said Vasya. "How cold it is in the night! Let us have tea, and I will go on again...."

"Do you feel better?"

"Yes, yes, I'm all right, I'm all right now."

"A happy New Year to you, brother Vasya."

"And to you too, brother, the same to you, dear boy."

They embraced each other. Vasya's chin was quivering and his eyes were moist. Arkady Ivanovitch was silent, he felt sad. They drank their tea hastily.

"Arkady, I've made up my mind, I am going myself to Yulian Mastakovitch."

"Why, he wouldn't notice——"

"But my conscience feels ill at ease, brother."

"But you know it's for his sake you are sitting here; it's for his sake you are wearing yourself out."

"Enough!"

"Do you know what, brother, I'll go round and see...."

"Whom?" asked Vasya.

"The Artemyevs. I'll take them your good wishes for the New Year as well as mine."

"My dear fellow! Well, I'll stay here; and I see it's a good idea of yours; I shall be working here, I shan't waste my time. Wait one minute, I'll write a note."

"Yes, do brother, do, there's plenty of time. I've still to wash and shave and to brush my best coat. Well, Vasya, we are going to be contented and happy. Embrace me, Vasya."

"Ah, if only we may, brother...."

"Does Mr. Shumkov live here?" they heard a child's voice on the stairs.

"Yes, my dear, yes," said Mavra, showing the visitor in.

"What's that? What is it?" cried Vasya, leaping up from the table and rushing to the entry, "Petinka, you?"

"Good morning, I have the honour to wish you a happy New Year, Vassily Petrovitch," said a pretty boy of ten years old with curly black hair. "Sister sends you her love, and so does Mamma, and Sister told me to give you a kiss for her."

Vasya caught the messenger up in the air and printed a long, enthusiastic kiss on his lips, which were very much like Lizanka's.

"Kiss him, Arkady," he said handing Petya to him, and without touching the ground the boy was transferred to Arkady Ivanovitch's powerful and eager arms.

"Will you have some breakfast, dear?"

"Thank-you, very much. We have had it already, we got up early to-day, the others have gone to church. Sister was two hours curling my hair, and pomading it, washing me and mending my trousers, for I tore them yesterday, playing with Sashka in the street, we were snowballing."

"Well, well, well!"

"So she dressed me up to come and see you, and then pomaded my head and then gave me a regular kissing. She said: 'Go to Vasya, wish him a happy New Year, and ask whether they are happy, whether they had a good night, and...' to ask something else, oh yes! whether you had finished the work you spoke of yesterday when you were there. Oh, I've got it all written down," said the boy, reading from a slip of paper which he took out of his pocket. "Yes, they were uneasy."

"It will be finished! It will be! Tell her that it will be. I shall finish it, on my word of honour!"

"And something else.... Oh yes, I forgot. Sister sent a little note and a present, and I was forgetting it!..."

"My goodness! Oh, you little darling! Where is it? where is it? That's it, oh! Look, brother, see what she writes. The dar–ling, the precious! You know I saw there yesterday a paper-case for me; it's not finished, so she says, 'I am sending you a lock of my hair, and the other will come later. Look, brother, look!"

And overwhelmed with rapture he showed Arkady Ivanovitch a curl of luxuriant, jet-black hair; then he kissed it fervently and put it in his breast pocket, nearest his heart.

"Vasya, I shall get you a locket for that curl," Arkady Ivanovitch said resolutely at last.

"And we are going to have hot veal, and to-morrow brains. Mamma wants to make cakes but we are not going to have millet porridge," said the boy, after a moment's thought, to wind up his budget of interesting items.

"Oh! what a pretty boy," cried Arkady Ivanovitch. "Vasya, you are the happiest of mortals."

The boy finished his tea, took from Vasya a note, a thousand kisses, and went out happy and frolicsome as before.

"Well, brother," began Arkady Ivanovitch, highly delighted, "you see how splendid it all is; you see. Everything is going well, don't be downcast, don't be uneasy. Go ahead! Get it done, Vasya, get it done. I'll be home at two o'clock. I'll go round to them, and then to Yulian Mastakovitch."

"Well, good-bye, brother; good-bye.... Oh! if only.... Very good, you go, very good," said Vasya, "then I really won't go to Yulian Mastakovitch."

"Good-bye."

"Stay, brother, stay, tell them well, whatever you think fit. Kiss her... and give me a full account of everything afterwards."

"Come, come–of course, I know all about it. This happiness has upset you. The suddenness of it all; you've not been yourself since yesterday. You have not got over the excitement of yesterday. Well, it's settled. Now try and get over it, Vasya. Good-bye, good-bye!"

At last the friends parted. All the morning Arkady Ivanovitch was preoccupied, and could think of nothing but Vasya. He knew his weak, highly nervous character. "Yes, this happiness has upset him, I was right there," he said to himself. "Upon my word, he has made me quite depressed, too, that man will make a tragedy of anything! What a feverish creature! Oh, I must save him! I must save him!" said Arkady, not noticing that he himself was exaggerating into something serious a slight trouble, in reality quite trivial. Only at eleven o'clock he reached the porter's lodge of Yulian Mastakovitch's house, to add his modest name to the long list of illustrious persons who had written their names on a sheet of blotted and scribbled paper in the porter's lodge. What was his surprise when he saw just above his own the signature of Vasya Shumkov! It amazed him. "What's the matter with him?" he thought. Arkady Ivanovitch, who had just been so buoyant with hope, came out feeling upset. There was certainly going to be trouble, but how? And in what form?

He reached the Artemyevs with gloomy forebodings; he seemed absent-minded from the first, and after talking a little with Lizanka went away with tears in his eyes; he was really anxious about Vasya. He went home running, and on the Neva came full tilt upon Vasya himself. The latter, too, was uneasy.

"Where are you going?" cried Arkady Ivanovitch.

Vasya stopped as though he had been caught in a crime.

"Oh, it's nothing, brother, I wanted to go for a walk."

"You could not stand it, and have been to the Artemyevs? Oh, Vasya, Vasya! Why did you go to Yulian Mastakovitch?"

Vasya did not answer, but then with a wave of his hand, he said: "Arkady, I don't know what is the matter with me. I...."

"Come, come, Vasya. I know what it is. Calm yourself. You've been excited, and overwrought ever since yesterday. Only think, it's not much to bear. Everybody's fond of you, everybody's ready to do anything for you; your work is getting on all right; you will get it done, you will certainly get it done. I know that you have been imagining something, you have had apprehensions about something.

"No, it's all right, it's all right...."

"Do you remember, Vasya, do you remember it was the same with you once before; do you remember, when you got your promotion, in your joy and thankfulness you were so zealous that you spoilt all your work for a week? It is just the same with you now."

"Yes, yes, Arkady; but now it is different, it is not that at all."

"How is it different? And very likely the work is not urgent at all, while you are killing yourself...."

"It's nothing, it's nothing. I am all right, it's nothing. Well, come along!"

"Why, are you going home, and not to them?"

"Yes, brother, how could I have the face to turn up there?... I have changed my mind. It was only that I could not stay on alone without you; now you are coming back with me I'll sit down to write again. Let us go!"

They walked along and for some time were silent. Vasya was in haste.

"Why don't you ask me about them?" said Arkady Ivanovitch.

"Oh, yes! Well, Arkasha, what about them?"

"Vasya, you are not like yourself."

"Oh, I am all right, I am all right. Tell me everything, Arkasha," said Vasya, in an imploring voice, as though to avoid further explanations. Arkady Ivanovitch sighed. He felt utterly at a loss, looking at Vasya.

His account of their friends roused Vasya. He even grew talkative. They had dinner together. Lizanka's mother had filled Arkady Ivanovitch's pockets with little cakes, and eating them the friends grew more cheerful. After dinner Vasya promised to take a nap, so as to sit up all night. He did, in fact, lie down. In the morning, some one whom it was impossible to refuse had invited Arkady Ivanovitch to tea. The friends parted. Arkady promised to come back as soon as he could, by eight o'clock if possible. The three hours of separation seemed to him like three years. At last he got away and rushed back to Vasya. When he went into the room, he found it in darkness. Vasya was not at home. He asked Mavra. Mavra said that he had been writing all the time, and had not slept at all, then he had paced up and down the room, and after that, an hour before, he had run out, saying he would be back in half-an-hour; "and when, says he, Arkady Ivanovitch comes in, tell him, old woman, says he," Mavra told him in conclusion, "that I have gone out for a walk," and he repeated the order three or four times.

"He is at the Artemyevs," thought Arkady Ivanovitch, and he shook his head.

A minute later he jumped up with renewed hope.

"He has simply finished," he thought, "that's all it is; he couldn't wait, but ran off there. But, no! he would have waited for me.... Let's have a peep what he has there."

He lighted a candle, and ran to Vasya's writing-table: the work had made progress and it looked as though there were not much left to do. Arkady Ivanovitch was about to investigate further, when Vasya himself walked in....

"Oh, you are here?" he cried, with a start of dismay.

Arkady Ivanovitch was silent. He was afraid to question Vasya. The latter dropped his eyes and. remained silent too, as he began sorting the papers. At last their eyes met. The look in Vasya's was so beseeching, imploring, and broken, that Arkady shuddered when he saw it. His heart quivered and was full.

"Vasya, my dear boy, what is it? What's wrong?" he cried, rushing to him and squeezing him in his arms. "Explain to me, I don't understand you, and your depression. What is the matter with you, my poor, tormented boy? What is it? Tell me all about it, without hiding anything. It can't be only this——"

Vasya held him tight and could say nothing. He could scarcely breathe.

"Don't, Vasya, don't! Well, if you don't finish it, what then? I don't understand you; tell me your trouble. You see it is for your sake I.... Oh dear! oh dear!" he said, walking up and down the room and clutching at everything he came across, as though seeking at once some remedy for Vasya. "I will go to Yulian Mastakovitch instead of you to-morrow. I will ask him–entreat him–to let you have another day. I will explain it all to him, anything, if it worries you So...."

"God forbid!" cried Vasya, and turned as white as the wall. He could scarcely stand on his feet.

"Vasya! Vasya!"

Vasya pulled himself together. His lips were quivering; he tried to say something, but could only convulsively squeeze Arkady's hand in silence. His hand was cold. Arkady stood facing him, full of anxious and miserable suspense. Vasya raised his eyes again.

"Vasya, God bless you, Vasya! You wring my heart, my dear boy, my friend."

Tears gushed from Vasya's eyes; he flung himself on Arkady's bosom.

"I have deceived you, Arkady," he said. "I have deceived you. Forgive me, forgive me! I have been faithless to your friendship...."

"What is it, Vasya? What is the matter?" asked Arkady, in real alarm.

"Look!"

And with a gesture of despair Vasya tossed out of the drawer on to the table six thick manuscripts, similar to the one he had copied.

"What's this?"

"What I have to get through by the day after to-morrow. I haven't done a quarter! Don't ask me, don't ask me how it has happened," Vasya went on, speaking at once of what was distressing him so terribly. "Arkady, dear friend, I don't know myself what came over me. I feel as though I were coming out of a dream. I have wasted three weeks doing nothing. I kept ... I kept going to see her.... My heart was aching, I was tormented by the uncertainty... I could not write. I did not even think about it. Only now, when happiness is at hand for me, I have come to my senses."

"Vasya," began Arkady Ivanovitch resolutely, "Vasya, I will save you. I understand it all. It's a serious matter; I will save you. Listen! listen to me: I will go to Yulian Mastakovitch to-morrow.... Don't shake your head; no, listen! I will tell him exactly how it has all been; let me do that... I will explain to him..... I will go into everything. I will tell him how crushed you are, how you are worrying yourself."

"Do you know that you are killing me now?" Vasya brought out, turning cold with horror.

Arkady Ivanovitch turned pale, but at once controlling himself, laughed.

"Is that all? Is that all?" he said. "Upon my word. Vasya, upon my word! Aren't you ashamed? Come, listen! I see that I am grieving you. You see I understand you; I know what is passing in your heart. Why, we have been living together for five years, thank God! You are such a kind, soft-hearted fellow, but weak. unpardonably weak. Why, even Lizaveta Mikalovna has noticed it. And you are a dreamer, and that's a bad thing, too; you may go from bad to worse, brother. I tell you, I know what you want! You would like Yulian Mastakovitch, for instance, to be beside himself and. maybe, to give a ball, too, from joy, because you are going to get married.... Stop, stop! you are frowning. You see that at one word from me you are offended on Yulian Mastakovitch's account. I'll let him alone. You know I respect him just as much as you do. But argue as you may, you can't prevent my thinking that you would like there to be no one unhappy in the whole world when you are getting married.... Yes, brother. you must admit that you would like me, for instance, your best friend, to come in for a fortune of a hundred thousand all of a sudden, you would like all the enemies in the world to be suddenly, for no rhyme or reason, reconciled, so that in their joy they might all embrace one another in the middle of the street, and then, perhaps, come here to call on you. Vasya, my dear boy, I am not laughing; it is true; you've said as much to me long ago, in different ways. Because you are happy, you want every one, absolutely every one, to become happy at once. It hurts you and troubles you to be happy alone. And so you want at once to do your utmost to be worthy of that happiness, and maybe to do some great deed to satisfy your conscience. Oh! I understand how ready you are to distress yourself for having suddenly been remiss just where you ought to have shown your zeal, your capacity... well, maybe your gratitude, as you say. It is very bitter for you to think that Yulian Mastakovitch may frown and even be angry when he sees that you have not justified the expectations he had of you. It hurts you to think that you may hear reproaches from the man you look upon as your benefactor-and at such a moment! when your heart is full of joy and you don't know on whom to lavish your gratitude.... Isn't that true? It is, isn't it?"

Arkady Ivanovitch, whose voice was trembling, paused, and drew a deep breath.

Vasya looked affectionately at his friend. A smile passed over his lips. His face even lighted up, as though with a gleam of hope.

"Well, listen, then," Arkady Ivanovitch began again, growing more hopeful, "there's no necessity that you should forfeit Yulian Mastakovitch's favour.... Is there, dear boy? Is there any question of it? And since it is so," said Arkady, jumping up, "I shall sacrifice myself for you. I am going to-morrow to Yulian Mastakovitch, and don't oppose me. You magnify your failure to a crime, Vasya. Yulian Mastakovitch is magnanimous and merciful, and, what is more, he is not like you. He will listen to you and me, and get us out of our trouble, brother Vasya. Well, are you calmer?"

Vasya pressed his friend's hands with tears in his eyes.

"Hush, hush, Arkady," he said, "the thing is settled. I haven't finished, so very well; if I haven't finished, I haven't finished, and there's no need for you to go. I will tell him all about it, I will go myself. I am calmer now, I am perfectly calm; only you mustn't go.... But listen...."

"Vasya, my dear boy," Arkady Ivanovitch cried joyfully, "I judged from what you said. I am glad that you have thought better of things and have recovered yourself. But whatever may befall you, whatever happens, I am with you, remember that. I see that it worries you to think of my speaking to Yulian Mastakovitch–and I won't say a word, not a word, you shall tell him yourself. You see, you shall go to-morrow.... Oh no, you had better not go, you'll go on writing here, you see, and I'll find out about this work, whether it is very urgent or not, whether it must be done by the time or not, and if you don't finish it in time what will come of it. Then I will run back to you. Do you see, do you see! There is still hope; suppose the work is not urgent–it may be all right. Yulian Mastakovitch may not remember, then all is saved."

Vasya shook his head doubtfully. But his grateful eyes never left his friend's face.

"Come, that's enough, I am so weak, so tired," he said, sighing. "I don't want to think about it. Let us talk of something else. I won't write either now; do you know I'll only finish two short pages just to get to the end of a passage. Listen I have long wanted to ask you, how is it you know me so well?"

Tears dropped from Vasya's eyes on Arkady's hand.

"If you knew, Vasya, how fond I am of you, you would not ask that–yes!"

"Yes, yes, Arkady, I don't know that, because I don't know why you are so fond of me. Yes, Arkady, do you know, even your love has been killing me? Do you know, ever so many times, particularly when I am thinking of you in bed (for I always think of you when I am falling asleep), I shed tears, and my heart throbs at the thought .. at the thought.... Well, at the thought that you are so fond of me, while I can do nothing to relieve my heart, can do nothing to repay you."

"You see, Vasya, you see what a fellow you are! Why, how upset you are now," said Arkady, whose heart ached at that moment and who remembered the scene in the street the day before.

"Nonsense, you want me to be calm, but I never have been so calm and happy! Do you know..... Listen, I want to tell you all about it, but I am afraid of wounding you.... You keep scolding me and being vexed; and I am afraid.... See how I am trembling now, I don't know why. You see, this is what I want to say. I feel as though I had never known myself before–yes! Yes, I only began to understand other people too, yesterday. I did not feel or appreciate things fully, brother. My heart .. was hard.... Listen how has it happened, that I have never done good to any one, any one in the world, because I couldn't–I am not even pleasant to look at.... But everybody does me good! You, to begin with: do you suppose I don't see that? Only I said nothing; only I said nothing."

"Hush, Vasya!"

"Oh, Arkasha! ... it's all right," Vasya interrupted, hardly able to articulate for tears. "I talked to you yesterday about Yulian Mastakovitch. And you know yourself how stern and severe he is, even you have come in for a reprimand from him; yet he deigned to jest with me yesterday, to show his affection, and kind-heartedness, which he prudently conceals from every one...."

"Come, Vasya, that only shows you deserve your good fortune."

"Oh, Arkasha! How I longed to finish all this.... No, I shall ruin my good luck! I feel that! Oh no, not through that," Vasya added, seeing that Arkady glanced at the heap of urgent work lying on the table, "that's nothing, that's only paper covered with writing it's nonsense! That matter's settled.... I went to see them to-day, Arkasha; I did not go in. I felt depressed and sad. I simply stood at the door. She was playing the piano, I listened. You see, Arkady," he went on, dropping his voice, "I did not dare to go in."

"I say, Vasya–what is the matter with you? You look at one so strangely."

"Oh, it's nothing. I feel a little sick; my legs are trembling; it's because I sat up last night. Yes! Everything looks green before my eyes. It's here, here——"

He pointed to his heart. He fainted. When he came to himself Arkady tried to take forcible measures. He tried to compel him to go to bed. Nothing would induce Vasya to consent. He shed tears, wrung his hands, wanted to write, was absolutely set on finishing his two pages. To avoid exciting him Arkady let him sit down to the work.

"Do you know," said Vasya, as he settled himself in his place, "an idea has occurred to me? There is hope."

He smiled to Arkady, and his pale face lighted up with a gleam of hope.

"I will take him what is done the day after to-morrow. About the rest I will tell a lie. I will say it has been burnt, that it has been sopped in water, that I have lost it.... That, in fact, I have not finished it; I cannot lie. I will explain, do you know, what? I'll explain to him all about it. I will tell him how it was that I could not. I'll tell him about my love; he has got married himself just lately, he'll understand me. I will do it all, of course, respectfully, quietly; he will see my tears and be touched by them...."

"Yes, of course, you must go, you must go and explain to him.... But there's no need of tears! Tears for what? Really, Vasya, you quite scare me."

"Yes, I'll go, I'll go. But now let me write, let me write, Arkasha. I am not interfering with any one, let me write!"

Arkady flung himself on the bed. He had no confidence in Vasya, no confidence at all. "Vasya was capable of anything, but to ask forgiveness for what? how? That was not the point. The point was, that Vasya had not carried out his obligations, that Vasya felt guilty in his own eyes, felt that he was ungrateful to destiny, that Vasya was crushed, overwhelmed by happiness and thought himself unworthy of it; that, in fact, he was simply trying to find an excuse to go off his head on that point, and that he had not recovered from the unexpectedness of what had happened the day before; that's what it is," thought Arkady Ivanovitch. "I must save him. I must reconcile him to himself. He will be his own ruin." He thought and thought, and resolved to go at once next day to Yulian Mastakovitch, and to tell him all about it.

Vasya was sitting writing. Arkady Ivanovitch, worn out, lay down to think things over again, and only woke at daybreak.

"Damnation! Again!" he cried, looking at Vasya; the latter was still sitting writing.

Arkady rushed up to him, seized him and forcibly put him to bed. Vasya was smiling: his eyes were closing with sleep. He could hardly speak.

"I wanted to go to bed," he said. "Do you know, Arkady, I have an idea; I shall finish. I made my pen go faster! I could not have sat at it any longer; wake me at eight o'clock."

Without finishing his sentence, he dropped asleep and slept like the dead.

"Mavra," said Arkady Ivanovitch to Mavra, who came in with the tea, "he asked to be waked in an hour. Don't wake him on any account! Let him sleep ten hours, if he can. Do you understand?"

"I understand, sir."

"Don't get the dinner, don't bring in the wood, don't make a noise or it will be the worse for you. If he asks for me, tell him I have gone to the office–do you understand?"

"I understand, bless you, sir; let him sleep and welcome! I am glad my gentlemen should sleep well, and I take good care of their things. And about that cup that was broken, and you blamed me, your honour, it wasn't me, it was poor pussy broke it, I ought to have kept an eye on her. 'S-sh, you confounded thing,' I said."

"Hush, be quiet, be quiet!"

Arkady Ivanovitch followed Mavra out into the kitchen, asked for the key and locked her up there. Then he went to the office. On the way he considered how he could present himself before Yulian Mastakovitch, and whether it would be appropriate and not impertinent. He went into the office timidly, and timidly inquired whether His Excellency were there; receiving the answer that he was not and would not be, Arkady Ivanovitch instantly thought of going to his flat, but reflected very prudently that if Yulian Mastakovitch had not come to the office he would certainly be busy at home. He remained. The hours seemed to him endless. Indirectly he inquired about the work entrusted to Shumkov, but no one knew anything about this. All that was known was that Yulian Mastakovitch did employ him on special jobs, but what they were–no one could say. At last it struck three o'clock, and Arkady Ivanovitch rushed out, eager to get home. In the vestibule he was met by a clerk, who told him that Vassily Petrovitch Shumkov had come about one o'clock and asked, the clerk added, "whether you were here, and whether Yulian Mastakovitch had been here." Hearing this Arkady Ivanovitch took a sledge and hastened home beside himself with alarm.

Shumkov was at home. He was walking about the room in violent excitement. Glancing at Arkady Ivanovitch, he immediately controlled himself, reflected, and hastened to conceal his emotion. He sat down to his papers without a word. He seemed to avoid his friend's questions, seemed to be bothered by them, to be pondering to himself on some plan, and deciding to conceal his decision, because he could not reckon further on his friend's affection. This struck Arkady, and his heart ached with a poignant and oppressive pain. He sat on the bed and began turning over the leaves of some book, the only one he had in his possession, keeping his eye on poor Vasya. But Vasya remained obstinately silent, writing, and not raising his head. So passed several hours, and Arkady's misery reached an extreme point. At last, at eleven o'clock, Vasya lifted his head and looked with a fixed, vacant stare at Arkady. Arkady waited. Two or three minutes passed; Vasya did not speak.

"Vasya!" cried Arkady.

Vasya made no answer.

"Vasya!" he repeated, jumping up from the bed, "Vasya, what is the matter with you? What is it?" he cried, running up to him.

Vasya raised his eyes and again looked at him with the same vacant, fixed stare.

"He's in a trance!" thought Arkady, trembling all over with fear. He seized a bottle of water, raised Vasya, poured some water on his head, moistened his temples, rubbed his hands in his own–and Vasya came to himself. "Vasya, Vasya!" cried Arkady, unable to restrain his tears. "Vasya, save yourself, rouse yourself, rouse yourself!..." He could say no more, but held him tight in his arms. A look as of some oppressive sensation passed over Vasya's face; he rubbed his forehead and clutched at his head, as though he were afraid it would burst.

"I don't know what is the matter with me," he added, at last. "I feel torn to pieces. Come, it's all right, it's all right! Give over, Arkady; don't grieve," he repeated, looking at him with sad, exhausted eyes.

"Why be so anxious? Come!"

"You, you comforting me!" cried Arkady, whose heart was torn. "Vasya," he said at last, "lie down and have a little nap, won't you? Don't wear yourself out for nothing! You'll set to work better afterwards."

"Yes, yes," said Vasya, "by all means, I'll lie down, very good. Yes! you see I meant to finish, but now I've changed my mind, yes...."

And Arkady led him to the bed.

"Listen, Vasya," he said firmly, "we must settle this matter finally. Tell me what were you thinking about?"

"Oh!" said Vasya, with a flourish of his weak hand turning over on the other side.

"Come, Vasya, come, make up your mind. I don't want to hurt you. I can't be silent any longer. You won't sleep till you've made up your mind, I know."

"As you like, as you like," Vasya repeated enigmatically.

"He will give in," thought Arkady Ivanovitch.

"Attend to me, Vasya," he said, "remember what I say, and I will save you to-morrow; to-morrow I will decide your fate! What am I saying, your fate? You have so frightened me, Vasya, that I am using your own words. Fate, indeed! It's simply nonsense, rubbish! You don't want to lose Yulian Mastakovitch's favour–affection, if you like. No! And you won't lose it, you will see. I——"

Arkady Ivanovitch would have said more, but Vasya interrupted him. He sat up in bed, put both arms round Arkady Ivanovitch's neck and kissed him. "Enough," he said in a weak voice, "enough! Say no more about that!"

And again he turned his face to the wall.

"My goodness!" thought Arkady, "my goodness! What is the matter with him? He is utterly lost. What has he in his mind! He will be his own undoing."

Arkady looked at him in despair.

"If he were to fall ill," thought Arkady, "perhaps it would be better. His trouble would pass off with illness, and that might be the best way of settling the whole business. But what nonsense I am talking. Oh, my God!"

Meanwhile Vasya seemed to be asleep. Arkady Ivanovitch was relieved. "A good sign," he thought.

He made up his mind to sit beside him all night. But Vasya was restless; he kept twitching and tossing about on the bed, and opening his eyes for an instant. At last exhaustion got the upper hand, he slept like the dead. It was about two o'clock in the morning, Arkady Ivanovitch began to doze in the chair with his elbow on the table!

He had a strange and agitated dream. He kept fancying that he was not asleep, and that Vasya was still lying on the bed. But strange to say, he fancied that Vasya was pretending, that he was deceiving him, that he was getting up, stealthily watching him out of the corner of his eye, and was stealing up to the writing table. Arkady felt a scalding pain at his heart; he felt vexed and sad and oppressed to see Vasya not trusting him, hiding and concealing himself from him. He tried to catch hold of him, to call out, to carry him to the bed. Then Vasya kept shrieking in his arms, and he laid on the bed a lifeless corpse. He opened his eyes and woke up; Vasya was sitting before him at the table, writing.

Hardly able to believe his senses, Arkady glanced at the bed; Vasya was not there. Arkady jumped up in a panic, still under the influence of his dream. Vasya did not stir; he went on writing. All at once Arkady noticed with horror that Vasya was moving a dry pen over the paper, was turning over perfectly blank pages, and hurrying, hurrying to fill up the paper as though he were doing his work in a most thorough and efficient way. "No, this is not a trance," thought Arkady Ivanovitch, and he trembled all over.

"Vasya, Vasya, speak to me," he cried, clutching him by the shoulder. But Vasya did not speak; he went on as before, scribbling with a dry pen over the paper.

"At last I have made the pen go faster," he said, without looking up at Arkady.

Arkady seized his hand and snatched away the pen.

A moan broke from Vasya. He dropped his hand and raised his eyes to Arkady; then with an air of misery and exhaustion he passed his hand over his forehead as though he wanted to shake off some leaden weight that was pressing upon his whole being, and slowly, as though lost in thought, he let his head sink on his breast.

"Vasya, Vasya!" cried Arkady in despair. "Vasya!"

A minute later Vasya looked at him, tears stood in his large blue eyes, and his pale, mild face wore a look of infinite suffering. He whispered something.

"What, what is it?" cried Arkady, bending down to him.

"What for, why are they doing it to me?" whispered Vasya. "What for? What have I done?"

"Vasya, what is it? What are you afraid of? What is it?" cried Arkady, wringing his hands in despair.

"Why are they sending me for a soldier?" said Vasya, looking his friend straight in the face. "Why is it? What have I done?"

Arkady's hair stood on end with horror; he refused to believe his ears. He stood over him, half dead.

A minute later he pulled himself together. "It's nothing, it's only for the minute," he said to himself, with pale face and blue, quivering lips, and he hastened to put on his outdoor things. He meant to run straight for a doctor. All at once Vasya called to him. Arkady rushed to him and clasped him in his arms like a mother whose child is being torn from her.

"Arkady, Arkady, don't tell any one! Don't tell any one, do you hear? It is my trouble, I must bear it alone."

"What is it–what is it? Rouse yourself, Vasya, rouse yourself!"

Vasya sighed, and slow tears trickled down his cheeks.

"Why kill her? How is she to blame?" he muttered in an agonized, heartrending voice. "The sin is mine, the sin is mine!"

He was silent for a moment.

"Farewell, my love! Farewell, my love!" he whispered, shaking his luckless head. Arkady started, pulled himself together and would have rushed for the doctor. "Let us go, it is time, cried Vasya, carried away by Arkady's last movement. "Let us go, brother, let us go; I am ready. You lead the way." He paused and looked at Arkady with a downcast and mistrustful face.

"Vasya, for goodness' sake, don't follow me! Wait for me here. I will come back to you directly, directly," said Arkady Ivanovitch, losing his head and snatching up his cap to run for a doctor. Vasya sat down at once, he was quiet and docile; but there was a gleam of some desperate resolution in his eye. Arkady turned back, snatched up from the table an open penknife, looked at the poor fellow for the last time, and ran out of the flat.

It was eight o'clock. It had been broad daylight for some time in the room.

He found no one. He was running about for a full hour. All the doctors whose addresses he had got from the house porter when he inquired of the latter whether there were no doctor living in the building, had gone out, either to their work or on their private affairs. There was one who saw patients. This one questioned at length and in detail the servant who announced that Nefedevitch had called, asking him who it was, from whom he came, what was the matter, and concluded by saying that he could not go, that he had a great deal to do, and that patients of that kind ought to be taken to a hospital.

Then Arkady, exhausted, agitated, and utterly taken aback by this turn of affairs, cursed all the doctors on earth, and rushed home in the utmost alarm about Vasya. He ran into the flat. Mavra, as though there were nothing the matter, went on scrubbing the floor, breaking up wood and preparing to light the stove. He went into the room; there was no trace of Vasya, he had gone out.

"Which way? Where? Where will the poor fellow be off to?" thought Arkady, frozen with terror. He began questioning Mavra. She knew nothing, had neither seen nor heard him go out, God bless him! Nefedevitch rushed off to the Artemyevs'.

It occurred to him for some reason that he must be there.

It was ten o'clock by the time he arrived. They did not expect him, knew nothing and had heard nothing. He stood before them frightened, distressed, and asked where was Vasya? The mother's legs gave way under her; she sank back on the sofa. Lizanka, trembling with alarm, began asking what had happened. What could he say? Arkady Ivanovitch got out of it as best he could, invented some tale which of course was not believed, and fled, leaving them distressed and anxious. He flew to his department that he might not be too late there, and he let them know that steps might be taken at once. On the way it occurred to him that Vasya would be at Yulian Mastakovitch's. That was more likely than anything: Arkady had thought of that first of all, even before the Artemyevs'. As he drove by His Excellency's door, he thought of stopping, but at once told the driver to go straight on. He made up his mind to try and find out whether anything had happened at the office, and if he were not there to go to His Excellency, ostensibly to report on Vasya. Some one must be informed of it.

As soon as he got into the waiting-room he was surrounded by fellow-clerks, for the most part young men of his own standing in the service. With one voice they began asking him what had happened to Vasya? At the same time they all told him that Vasya had gone out of his mind, and thought that he was to be sent for a soldier as a punishment for having neglected his work. Arkady Ivanovitch, answering them in all directions, or rather avoiding giving a direct answer to any one, rushed into the inner room. On the way he learned that Vasya was in Yulian Mastakovitch's private room, that every one had been there and that Esper Ivanovitch had gone in there too. He was stopped on the way. One of the senior clerks asked him who he was and what he wanted? Without distinguishing the person he said something about Vasya and went straight into the room. He heard Yulian Mastakovitch's voice from within. "Where are you going?" some one asked him at the very door. Arkady Ivanovitch was almost in despair; he was on the point of turning back, but through the open door he saw his poor Vasya. He pushed the door and squeezed his way into the room. Every one seemed to be in confusion and perplexity, because Yulian Mastakovitch was apparently much chagrined. All the more important personages were standing about him talking, and coming to no decision. At a little distance stood

Vasya. Arkady's heart sank when he looked at him. Vasya was standing, pale, with his head up, stiffly erect, like a recruit before a new officer, with his feet together and his hands held rigidly at his sides. He was looking Yulian Mastakovitch straight in the face. Arkady was noticed at once, and some one who knew that they lodged together mentioned the fact to His Excellency. Arkady was led up to him. He tried to make some answer to the questions put to him, glanced at Yulian Mastakovitch and seeing on his face a look of genuine compassion, began trembling and sobbing like a child. He even did more, he snatched His Excellency's hand and held it to his eyes, wetting it with his tears, so that Yulian Mastakovitch was obliged to draw it hastily away, and waving it in the air, said, "Come, my dear fellow, come! I see you have a good heart." Arkady sobbed and turned an imploring look on every one. It seemed to him that they were all brothers of his dear Vasya, that they were all worried and weeping about him. "How, how has it happened? how has it happened?" asked Yulian Mastakovitch.

"What has sent him out of his mind?"

"Gra–gra–gratitude!" was all Arkady Ivanovitch could articulate.

Every one heard his answer with amazement, and it seemed strange and incredible to every one that a man could go out of his mind from gratitude. Arkady explained as best he could.

"Good Heavens! what a pity!" said Yulian Mastakovitch at last. "And the work entrusted to him was not important, and not urgent in the least. It was not worth while for a man to kill himself over it! Well, take him away!"... At this point Yulian Mastakovitch turned to Arkady Ivanovitch again, and began questioning him once more. "He begs," he said, pointing to Vasya, "that some girl should not be told of this. Who is she–his betrothed, I suppose?"

Arkady began to explain. Meanwhile Vasya seemed to be thinking of something, as though he were straining his memory to the utmost to recall some important, necessary matter, which was particularly wanted at this moment. From time to time he looked round with a distressed face, as though hoping some one would remind him of what he had forgotten. He fastened his eyes on Arkady. All of a sudden there was a gleam of hope in his eyes; he moved with the left leg forward, took three steps as smartly as he could, clicking with his right boot as soldiers do when they move forward at the call from their officer. Every one was waiting to see what would happen.

"I have a physical defect and am small and weak, and I am not fit for military service, Your Excellency," he said abruptly.

At that every one in the room felt a pang at his heart, and firm as was Yulian Mastakovitch's character, tears trickled from his eyes.

"Take him away," he said, with a wave of his hands.

"Present!" said Vasya in an undertone; he wheeled round to the left and marched out of the room. All who were interested in his fate followed him out. Arkady pushed his way out behind the others. They made Vasya sit down in the waiting-room till the carriage came which had been ordered to take him to the hospital. He sat down in silence and seemed in great anxiety. He nodded to any one he recognized as though saying good-bye. He looked round towards the door every minute, and prepared himself to set off when he should be told it was time. People crowded in a close circle round him; they were all shaking their heads and lamenting. Many of them were much impressed by his story, which had suddenly become known. Some discussed his illness, while others expressed their pity and high opinion of Vasya, saying that he was such a quiet, modest young man, that he had been so promising; people described what efforts he had made to learn, how eager he was for knowledge, how he had worked to educate himself. "He had risen by his own efforts from a humble position," some one observed. They spoke with emotion of His Excellency's affection for him. Some of them fell to explaining why Vasya was possessed by the idea that he was being sent for a soldier, because he had not finished his work. They said that the poor fellow had so lately belonged to the class liable for military service and had only received his first grade through the good offices of Yulian Mastakovitch, who had had the cleverness to discover his talent, his docility, and the rare mildness of his disposition. In fact, there was a great number of views and theories.

A very short fellow-clerk of Vasya's was conspicuous as being particularly distressed. He was not very young, probably about thirty. He was pale as a sheet, trembling all over and smiling queerly, perhaps because any scandalous affair or terrible scene both frightens, and at the same time somewhat rejoices the outside spectator. He kept running round the circle that surrounded Vasya, and as he was so short, stood on tiptoe and caught at the button of every one–that is, of those with whom he felt entitled to take such a liberty–and kept saying that he knew how it had all happened, that it was not so simple, but a very important matter, that it couldn't be left without further inquiry; then stood on tiptoe again, whispered in some one's ear, nodded his head again two or three times, and ran round again. At last everything was over. The porter made his appearance, and an attendant from the hospital went up to Vasya and told him it was time to start. Vasya jumped up in a flutter and went with them, looking about him. He was looking about for some one.

"Vasya, Vasya!" cried Arkady Ivanovitch, sobbing. Vasya stopped, and Arkady squeezed his way up to him. They flung themselves into each other's arms in a last bitter embrace. It was sad to see them. What monstrous calamity was wringing the tears from their eyes! What were they weeping for? What was their trouble? Why did they not understand one another?

"Here, here, take it! Take care of it," said Shumkov, thrusting a paper of some kind into Arkady's hand. "They will take it away from me. Bring it me later on; bring it ... take care of it...." Vasya could not finish, they called to him. He ran hurriedly downstairs, nodding to every one, saying good-bye to every one. There was despair in his face. At last he was put in the carriage and taken away. Arkady made haste to open the paper: it was Liza's curl of black hair, from which Vasya had never parted. Hot tears gushed from Arkady's eyes: oh, poor Liza!

When office hours were over, he went to the Artemyevs'. There is no need to describe what happened there! Even Petya, little Petya, though he could not quite understand what had happened to dear Vasya, went into a corner, hid his face in his little hands, and sobbed in the fullness of his childish heart. It was quite dusk when Arkady returned home. When he reached the Neva he stood still for a minute and turned a keen glance up the river into the smoky frozen thickness of the distance, which was suddenly flushed crimson with the last purple and blood-red glow of sunset, still smouldering on the misty horizon.... Night lay over the city, and the wide plain of the Neva, swollen with frozen snow, was shining in the last gleams of the sun with myriads of sparks of gleaming hoar frost. There was a frost of twenty degrees. A cloud of frozen steam hung about the overdriven horses and the hurrying people. The condensed atmosphere quivered at the slightest sound, and from all the roofs on both sides of the river, columns of smoke rose up like giants and floated across the cold sky, intertwining and untwining as they went, so that it seemed new buildings were rising up above the old, a new town was taking shape in the air.... It seemed as if all that world, with all its inhabitants, strong and weak, with all their habitations, the refuges of the poor, or the gilded palaces for the comfort of the powerful of this world was at that twilight hour like a fantastic vision of fairy-land, like a dream which in its turn would vanish and pass away like vapour into the dark blue sky. A strange thought came to poor Vasya's forlorn friend. He started, and his heart seemed at that instant flooded with a hot rush of blood kindled by a powerful, overwhelming sensation he had never known before. He seemed only now to understand all the trouble, and to know why his poor Vasya had gone out of his mind, unable to bear his happiness. His lips twitched, his eyes lighted up, he turned pale, and as it were had a clear vision into something new.

He became gloomy and depressed, and lost all his gaiety. His old lodging grew hateful to him–he took a new room. He did not care to visit the Artemyevs, and indeed he could not. Two years later he met Lizanka in church. She was by then married; beside her walked a wet nurse with a tiny baby. They greeted each other, and for a long time avoided all mention of the past. Liza said that, thank God, she was happy, that she was not badly off, that her husband was a kind man and that she was fond of him.... But suddenly in the middle of a sentence her eyes filled with tears, her voice failed, she turned away, and bowed down to the church pavement to hide her grief.